THE McGILLICUDDY BOOK OF PERSONAL RECORDS

THE McGILLICUDDY BOOK OF PERSONAL RECORDS

Colleen Sydor

Red Deer PRESS

Published by
Red Deer Press
A Fitzhenry & Whiteside Company
195 Allstate Parkway,
Markham, ON L3R 4T8
www.reddeerpress.com

Credits
Edited by Peter Carver
Text design by Tanya Montini
Cover design by Jacquie Morris & Delta Embree, Liverpool, Nova Scotia
Printed and bound in Canada

Acknowledgments
Financial support provided by the Canada Council, and the Government of Canada through
the Book Publishing Industry Development Program (BPIDP).

Canada Council   Conseil des Arts
for the Arts   du Canada

ONTARIO ARTS COUNCIL
CONSEIL DES ARTS DE L'ONTARIO

Library and Archives Canada Cataloguing in Publication
Sydor, Colleen
The McGillicuddy book of personal records / Colleen Sydor.
ISBN 978-0-88995-434-2
I. Title.
PS8587.Y36M34 2010   jC813'.54   C2010-900197-4

Publisher Cataloging-in-Publication Data (U.S)
Sydor Colleen.
The McGillicuddy book of personal records / Colleen Sydor.
[256] p. : cm.

ISBN: 978-0-88995-434-2 (pbk.)
1. Friendship – Fiction. 2. Courage – Fiction. I. Title.
[Fic] dc22   PZ7.S936Mb 2010

ANCIENT FOREST™
FRIENDLY

38
trees were saved
for our forests

Preserving our environment
Red Deer Press chose to print the pages of this
book on recycled paper and saved these resources:

energy	water	greenhouse gases	solid waste
12 million BTUs	65,310 L	1,625 kg	476 kg

Printed by **Webcom Inc.** on
Legacy Hi-Bulk Natural 100% post-consumer waste.

01 11

mental Defense Paper Calculator.

FSC

Mixed Sources
Product group from well-managed
forests, controlled sources and
recycled wood or fiber

Cert no. SW-COC-002358
www.fsc.org
© 1996 Forest Stewardship Council

Do your work with mastery.

Like the moon, come out from behind the clouds!

Shine.

– *Buddha*

One must never let the fire go out in one's soul,

but keep it burning.

– *Vincent van Gogh*

Hide it under a bushel?

No! I'm gonna let it shine.

– *Author unknown*

I would like to acknowledge and thank the following friends for their generous contributions to this book and for their collective wisdom: Albert Einstein, Leonardo da Vinci, Mahatama Gandhi, Emily Dickinson, Groucho Marx, William Shakespeare, the Dalai Lama, Mark Twain, Plato, William Blake, Charlie Chaplin, Charlie Brown, Buddha, Vincent van Gogh, e. e. cummings, Confucius, Robert Frost, & Connie Mack.

A million thanks, guys!

For Sue, who knew

"Hi, Daddy."

"*Jeez*, Rhonda," said Lee, "how many times do I have to tell you not to sneak up ..."

Rhonda interrupted him like she always did. "I've told you a *zillion* times not to call me that," she said. "My name's Ron."

"Yeah, and mine's Lee, but that doesn't stop you from calling me Daddy. And I've told *you* a zillion and *ten* times."

He'd earned the nickname at school after taking on a growth spurt that left him a good six inches taller than the tallest kid in the class. Daddy. Short for Daddy Long Legs. And he definitely had them—long legs, that is. Lee had become used to the name ages ago, but he knew he'd never get used to Rhonda calling him that. Not only was Rhonda three years younger than Lee, but she was as short for her age as Lee was tall. It was just a little too creepy to have a pygmy ten-year-old following you around all the time calling you Daddy.

"Thought you quit the basketball team," said Rhonda.

Lee knew her fingertips were fairly itching to grab the ball and make him chase her. He backed away a step or two. "You can't quit a team you've never been on," said Lee. "You know very well I got cut the first day."

It hadn't been his idea, by the way—trying out for the basketball team. He'd given in to everyone's hounding just to get them off his back. But he knew it would be a disaster. Just because a guy towers above everyone else on the court doesn't mean he'll be a natural at ker-plunking or splunking or whatever the heck they called it. *Slam-dunking*, that was it. And he'd tried telling them as much. But no. They'd forced him to prove his klutziness to an entire gym full of people instead. *Kathunk kathunk kathunk.*

"So if you're not on the team, then why ya practicing?"

"I'm not practicing."

"Yes, you are."

"No, I'm not."

"Yes, you are."

"No, I'm n …" Lee stopped himself just in time to save his dignity. Rhonda waited for him to finish the sentence, then became impatient.

"What *are* you doing, then?"

He started to answer, then stopped again. Rhonda had a way of making him forget that he didn't owe her any explanations. Why was he always baring his soul to this kid?

"Oh, I get it," said Rhonda, giving her nose an upward swipe with the heel of her hand. The habit had left a permanent pale crease above the tip of her nose. Lee liked to tease her about it when he was in a generous mood. Rhonda spoke up. "You're breaking another one of your dumb old records, aren't ya?"

Lee didn't answer. She was ruining his focus. Like she always did. And how the heck had she found him here, anyhow? He'd calculated that this abandoned garage lot was far enough away from school to avoid curious, smart-alecky onlookers. But that was Rhonda all over—she seemed to be able to sniff him out like a hound dog.

Lee continued to bounce the ball with a look of severe concentration so maybe she'd get the message and vamoose. No such luck.

"Going for the full twelve hours this time?"

Some records required only skill (or stupidity), and could be over in a few seconds. It didn't take long to swallow fifty live goldfish, for example. But others required time and mega patience, and those were his specialties. Most of Lee's records were limited to twelve hours, max. It was the longest stretch of time he could stay out of the house and not get hauled back home for dinner, or bed, or something equally lame. If he started at nine in the morning, and told his mother he was staying at a friend's place for lunch and supper, he could still make it home by nine in the evening—his curfew time. Last time he'd done the basketball challenge, he'd only lasted ten hours and thirteen minutes. He'd tried peeing while bouncing the ball at the same time, but it had ended badly, and his mother gave him heck for dribbling in the *bathroom*, of all places. (The *basketball* kind of dribbling, you understand.) This time he was prepared. He hadn't had anything to drink since yesterday afternoon and, if worse came to worst, there was always the bushes.

"Ignore me if you want," said Rhonda, "but if you do, I won't go away."

He knew she meant it. "I'm trying to break ten hours, thirteen," he muttered. Then he looked her straight in the eye. "Bye *bye*, now!"

Rhonda ignored him. She stopped watching the basketball and turned her attention to a tattoo on her forearm—fake, of course. It was half peeled off so you couldn't even tell what it was anymore. The tattoo was one of six applied four weeks ago.

Made Lee wonder how often she bathed ...

Rhonda "Ron" Ronaldson of Winnipeg, Manitoba, sets an ALL-TIME PERSONAL RECORD for the longest stretch of consecutive days without taking a bath—twelve weeks, six days, ten hours, and counting. Miss Ronaldson is also trying for a simultaneous record of how much mud one person can pack under her fingernails at one time ...

Lee could suddenly feel Rhonda's eyes boring into him. "Why are you smirking to yourself?" she said, "What goes on in that pea-brain of yours?" Lee refused to reply, so she came up with a question he was more likely to answer. "Staying at Gertie's or Aggie's tonight?" she asked, picking at the last letter of what used to spell *Rebel* across her bicep (if you could call it that).

"Gertie's working tonight," he answered. "*Jeez*, now look at that, Ron," he said, exasperated. "You've got me calling my own mother Gertie. Why can't you just say 'your mom' like any normal person?"

Ron shrugged her shoulders without looking at him. She stared at her not-quite-immaculate fingernails, zeroing in on which one to bite first. She settled on a hangnail on the side of her thumb.

"And you'd better not let Agnes catch you calling her Aggie," warned Lee, "or she'll string you up by your boxers." Rhonda pulled the waistband of her boy's underwear above the tops of her jeans. She liked to advertise them that way.

Agnes was Lee's neighbor. And his other mother. From time to time, his *real* mother worked the late shift as a bouncer at the All Night Country and Western Club, and on those nights he ate and slept at Agnes's. The rest of the time he lived at home. It made him think of the kids at school who had divorced parents— spending so many days a week at Dad's house, so many at Mom's. Lee didn't have a dad, so in some ways it wasn't so bad having two moms. And Agnes was more than willing to fill the position. She didn't even charge money anymore. Said he was like a son to her, and since she didn't have any kids of her own, Gertrude was the one doing *her* the favor, not the other way around. He figured that's why she called him Sonny most of the time. Agnes insisted it was Sunny with a "u" but he knew she said it with an "o." Lee, Sonny, Daddy. Three names, two mothers. And one annoying short kid who worshiped the ground he walked on (heck, yeah, he'd figured that one out for himself ages ago). And Rhonda might just as well have been one of Agnes's kids as well, for all the time she spent hanging around there.

"Maybe I'll see you at Aggie's later," she said, faking a yawn. She pounced toward Lee as if to grab the basketball and just about gave him a heart attack; he came that close to losing control of the ball. She laughed as she took off down the street toward home. Lee shook his head.

RECORD OF THE CENTURY held by Lee "Daddy" "Sonny" McGillicuddy of 933 Dorchester Avenue for putting up with a scrawny, pain-in-the-butt, tomboy turkey bugging him every second of the day—a grueling four years, twelve weeks, and who knows how many days—basically, ever since she moved into the rundown house across the street.

With Rhonda finally gone, it felt like a giant relief to be alone again. For about an hour. Then the boredom started to set in. It would have been good to have *anyone* around then—even Rhonda Ronaldson. Lee thought about Santiago at home on her leash, waiting patiently for him. This morning, before leaving, he'd whispered in her ear that she'd have to be extra patient today, that he had something important he had to do. Boy, what he wouldn't give to see her slobbery jowls and wagging tail right now, but he knew she'd only want to play, and that just wouldn't do.

Kathunk, kathunk. This was the hard part, when the boredom made you want to pack it all in. Worst thing was, he knew the hardest part was yet to come—boredom *and* pain mixed together. Aching back, tired feet, sore wrists. By that point, the basketball would cease to be a basketball and become his worst enemy. *Kathunk, kathunk.* The mere sound of it smacking the pavement over and over and over again could make him want to puncture the stupid thing with a jackknife and stomp the life out of it until it was flat as one of Agnes's failed cakes. Yeah, that's just about when he'd start to question his own sanity. Was he nuts? What was the point of all this? Why not go home to a warm supper and a hot bath? And he'd be tempted to do just that if he didn't know something else ... that there'd be that amazing point when he'd get past the boredom and the pain, when his will gave him wings to ...

Lee heard footsteps and the unmistakable clink of a dog leash approaching. Could it be Rhonda bringing Santiago for a visit? He watched, disappointed, as an old man walked by with a mutt nowhere near as gorgeous as Santi. Lee sighed. Just for a little variety, he began bouncing the basketball closer to the ground. *Thunka-thunka-thunka.* He liked how the quick, short bounces sped things up, made him feel like time was passing faster. Anything to make him forget his full bladder. So much for not drinking anything for the last twelve hours. Lee figured it was the dehydration combined with an empty stomach and a full day in the hot sun that was making him feel kind of nauseous. And dizzy. The faster he bounced the ball, the worse it got. He straightened up and went for a series of high slow bounces. That helped a little with the queasiness, but did nothing for his screaming bladder.

Lee looked over at the bushes. Crap. He didn't trust his coordination for this right now. His hands felt shaky. And clammy, too—that wasn't good for basketball grip at the best of times. And it would mean moving from the pavement onto the long grass. Lee looked around. Better get this over with. As he stepped from the pavement of the empty parking lot into the weedy grass, the muffled sound of the bouncing made him feel weird, as if he were walking into a dream. That, mixed with the light-headedness, made him think he was losing it. That's pretty much when the lights went out. The last thing Lee remembered as he crumpled onto the grass was a wonderful feeling of flooding warmth. No, not so wonderful. *McGillicuddy boy pees pants, setting a new record in personal humiliation.* That was Lee's last thought before conking out cold.

CHAPTER TWO

{
**It's not whether you get knocked down;
it's whether you get up.**
– Vince Lombardi
}

Heck is *that*? A warm, wet washcloth—a warm, wet, *stinky* washcloth wiping his face over and over again. What the hey? Lee opened one eye to find Santiago licking the devil out of his left cheek. And Rhonda slapping the daylights out of his right cheek. "Daddy, Daddy, you o*kay*?"

"Knock it off, Ron," he said, pushing her away. Lee raised himself on one elbow. "What are you doing here?" he squinted at the unfamiliar bushes. "Where the heck am I?"

"You fainted!" said Rhonda. "I was just bringing Santiago over for a visit and I saw you keel right over. You okay?"

Lee sat up. "'*Course* I'm okay." Then he lay back down. He wasn't okay. He was sure he was going to throw up. He was already lying there in front of Rhonda Ronaldson, in wet Levis. Now all he needed was to upchuck in front of her. The smell of Santiago's dog breath wasn't helping.

"Just give me a minute," he said.

Rhonda settled back on her haunches and watched Santiago sniffing at Lee's wet jeans. When she caught Lee noticing the *sucks-to-be-you* look on her face, she turned away fast and whistled a tune into the treetops.

Smooth as sandpaper Ronaldson, thought Lee. He rolled his eyeballs. *Ouch!* That gave him a headache. He took a deep breath and slowly stood up. Bed. He wanted his bed.

Unfortunately, *bed* happened to be three blocks away.

"Do you need help?" asked Rhonda.

"No," said Lee. A wave of dizziness. "Yes."

Rhonda took his arm and steadied him as he weaved his way down the sidewalk. "What happened, anyway?" she asked.

"Sunstroke, probably," he said. "Had it before, once. Should have worn a baseball cap, I guess."

Three blocks might as well have been three miles, as far as Lee was concerned. And as they approached his street, his brain was such a bowl of mush he couldn't even remember which "home" he was staying at tonight—pfffff! which was mostly his *mother's* fault; how was he supposed to keep track of her constantly changing schedule. He'd asked her once why she couldn't just work Monday to Friday like the rest of the world, and she'd snorted, "The day I become a creature of habit is the day I make like a lemming and head for the nearest cliff."

"Just lead me to the nearest cliff," he mumbled to Rhonda, "and make it a high one." But instead, he felt her steering him toward Agnes's house. Good, thought Lee, Agnes would be the better of the two moms tonight. He knew his real mother would have a thing or two to say about this, and he didn't have the stomach for it right now. Didn't it just figure that as they reached Agnes's sidewalk, his mother came bustling out of her own front door, late for work. She was tucking her denim shirt into her blue jeans with one hand and straightening her cowboy hat with the other. She stopped dead when she saw Lee leaning on Rhonda, looking pale as a naked spud. Lee used his last ounce of energy to make it up the steps and into Agnes's house.

"What's up with him?" Gertrude asked Rhonda as they both followed him into the house.

"Sunstroke," said Rhonda.

"*Sun*stroke," repeated Gertrude, hurrying over to the couch where Agnes was already fussing over Lee. "I thought you were going to a movie with a friend today." She put a hand to his forehead. "How can you get sunstroke in an air-conditioned movie theater?" Her look of concern suddenly changed to one of suspicion. "Lee," said Gertrude, eyes narrowed, "*please*, tell me you weren't doing another one of your fool marathon records again ..."

Lee knew his mother wasn't going to like this. He remembered the day she finally put her foot down and tried to squash his record-breaking stunts. It had been a rainy afternoon when she'd come home from work to find him in the kitchen on his pogo stick. He happened to be two hours and eighteen minutes into a record of non-stop bouncing and the linoleum still had the dents to prove it. There had been no need for his mother to say a word. He could translate the angry smoke signals that had poured from her red ears that day: *Verboten*. No more records. The end. And now here he was with sunstroke.

Lee looked up now at his mother's broad shoulders. There was a reason she'd been hired as a security bouncer at the Country and Western. Aside from her size, she had a presence that let you know at once that she wasn't about to put up with any monkey business. Lee had heard stories of grown men who had been known to cower past her and out the club door after merely receiving one of her "I think it's about time you were heading home" looks. Lee knew she had a soft side, but not everyone did.

"Your lipstick's on crooked," said Lee, hoping to buy a little time. Gertrude always wore a bold swipe of lipstick the same color as her bright red neckerchief.

"Never mind that," said his mother. "Didn't I make it *abun*dantly clear to you that …"

But Lee was gone. He just made it to the bathroom in time.

Rhonda squeezed her eyes shut and wrinkled her nose as she heard him retch.

Gertrude sighed, went to the kitchen for a cool cloth to put on Lee's forehead, and met him at the bathroom door. "Come on, kiddo," she said, gently leading him down the narrow hall to his bedroom.

Agnes grabbed a plate of homemade gingersnaps, and she and Rhonda tailed Gertrude (well ... more accurately, Agnes tailed Gert, and Rhonda tailed the plate of cookies) and squeezed in the door before Gert could shut it.

By this time, Lee was moderately confident that the danger of barfing in front of them had passed. He looked at the trio at the foot of his bed and imagined he was viewing them through the lens of a video camera—zoom in for a close-up of their faces, zoom back out for a full frontal view of three goofy people framed against his bedroom wall like some kind of wacky portrait—okay, hold it; now freeze that frame. If he weren't feeling so crappy, he'd be tempted to laugh at this bizarre picture of extremes: Rhonda, as short as he was tall, Agnes as thin as his mother was wide. It was as if they were made of silly putty and some kid had come along and stretched them this way and that for his own crazy amusement. It seemed to Lee that life was all about extremes. At school, for example. Kids were either very cool, or way uncool. They either came from nauseatingly normal families, or totally weird ones. Sometimes Lee wished he could just be Joe Average—dive right into the mainstream and coast along the current with everybody else. More often, though, the thought of being "ordinary" seemed like the worst life sentence in the world.

Agnes plumped his pillow, then sat on the edge of his bed and offered him a cookie. Aggie was every bit as strict as his mom, but she didn't mind letting her affection gush out in a way that would have embarrassed his mother.

"You sure you don't mind, Agnes?" said Gertrude. "Because I can book off work if you'd rather—"

"'Course I don't mind," chirped Agnes. "Sonny'll be just fine here with me." She looked over her shoulder at Gertrude. "Run along, now. No point in being late for work."

Lee could see the motherly apprehension on Gertrude's face as she took his chin in her fingers and gazed into his eyes as if she could read something there. Lee didn't know much about telepathy, but just in case, he imagined his eyes were computer screens with the words I'LL BE FINE!! written across them in bold. Lee's mom must have picked up the message. Suddenly satisfied, she squeezed Lee's toe on her way out, and she and Agnes left the room, discussing such details as whether or not the ginger ale supplies would hold out until morning, and whether it wouldn't be a good idea to persuade him to take a Gravol.

CHAPTER THREE

Rhonda took two more cookies from the plate beside Lee's bed and fed one to Santiago. Lee could see she was enjoying this. *He* knew that *she* knew that the sign on his bedroom door, *STAY OUT OR DIE!!* was specifically meant for her. He also knew how much that bugged her. And now, here she was making a slow tour of his room with a smug smile while he watched, helpless, from his bed. There was nothing he could do about it. He was too sick to get up and kick her out. Besides, she *had* more or less helped him out this afternoon—although he guessed that that would have its own drawbacks. Tomorrow she'd be announcing to the world that she'd saved Daddy McGillicuddy's life.

"This as nice as your bedroom at Gertie's?" she asked. He'd made sure she'd never poked her nose inside that bedroom, either.

Lee shrugged his shoulders. "'Bout the same."

Rhonda pointed to a framed photograph on the wall. "That your decreased father or sumthin'?"

Lee sat upright. "The word is *deceased*, ya blockhead!" he said, "and *no*, that is not my dad. It just happens to be the one and only Albert Einstein, the Father of Relativity. Cheeeez!"

Rhonda shrugged. "Least he's *some*body's father." She ambled over to his desk and took a leisurely look at the stuff heaped there: three old Eatmore wrappers, a dirty hacky sack that looked like it had landed in Santiago's dinner bowl (or worse), and a half-eaten sandwich of peanut butter and ... something red.

"Peanut butter and *ketchup*?" she said, faking a gag.

Lee rolled on his side, clutching his stomach. "Come on," he groaned, "give a guy a break." She picked up a crumpled English essay, flattened it out, and looked at the mark on the last page—c-minus. She re-scrunched it and picked up something else. "What was his name, anyhow?"

"Whose?"

"Your decreased ... I mean, your dead dad."

Long pause. "Frankin," said Lee wearily—he knew what was coming.

"Frankin?" She let out a hoot. "As in, like ... *Frankin*stein?"

"No," said an impatient Lee, "Frankin is short for *frankin*cense ... you know, gold, frankincense, and myrrh? He was born on Christmas Day—what can I say?" Lee rolled over so his back faced Rhonda. "Mostly people just called him Frankinstein, though." He didn't bother spilling the fact that his own nickname for his dad had been Frankindad.

"Yeah, okay, so what's this?" said Rhonda, grown tired of the subject. She held up a small wooden plaque with a smooth black stone glued to its center.

"Black Cat," mumbled Lee into his pillow.

"That some kind of precious stone, or what?"

"Black Cat *bub*ble gum, bozo," he said. "When I was nine, I chewed that piece eight hours every day for exactly one year." Lee rolled onto his back and rubbed his stomach in a slow circular motion the way his mother used to when he was a kid with a bellyache. He could suddenly taste Black Cat in the back of his throat, and it made him wish the stuff had never been invented. "Can we drop the food references?" he said.

That's not all Rhonda let drop. The plaque fell from her fingers like a hot potato.

"Hey! Careful," said Lee. Rhonda wiped her hands on the back of her jeans as if she'd just picked up someone's wet Kleenex by mistake.

"Hey, neato," she said, once she'd recovered. "Where'd you get this?" She was looking up at a poster on his wall that said: THIS IS YOUR BRAIN. THIS IS YOUR BRAIN ON DRUGS. "Shoot," she said, trying to cover the picture of a fried egg for the sake of Lee's stomach. But it was no good. Even if Lee couldn't see the egg, he could remember the snot-like, membrany, slippy-slidy egg innards of every egg he'd ever cracked in his life. He covered his head with his pillow.

"Sorry," said Rhonda. She sat down at his computer and he

heard her tapping away, clicking with the mouse.

"What're you doing?"

"Nothing."

*&@#@**#!! He badly wished she'd go and do *nothing* someplace else!

Instead, Rhonda ran a finger down the ribs of his perfectly stacked CDs, and along the spines of the books on his shelf. Lee knew it irritated Rhonda that he seemed always to have his nose stuck in a book. Once she'd grabbed a hardcover novel out of his hand and cranged him over the head with it. To get back at her, he'd shot her one of the many famous sayings he had stored in his head (another habit of his that bugged her butt)—"Groucho Marx once said: 'Outside of a dog, a book is a man's best friend. Inside of a dog, it's too dark to read.'" Lee smiled now to think how grouchy that had made her.

Rhonda snatched a book from the shelf. "Hemingway, huh? La-*dee*-da." Rhonda fanned through the pages. "This crappy, or what?"

"*The Old Man and the Sea?*" Lee peeked out from under his pillow. "You haven't read it?"

"Nope."

Lee patted the side of his bed and whistled for his dog, "Come on, girl, up you come." Santiago jumped up and tried licking Lee's face. "My dad named Santiago after the guy in that book. He read it to me twice before he ..." Lee hated using the word *died*. It somehow seemed like one of those embarrassing words not to be used in mixed company. For once he was glad when Rhonda cut him off.

. "Whoa, back up. Your dad named your female dog after an *old man*?"

"Give it here," said Lee, reaching for the book as if to rescue it. It was worn and dog-eared. He didn't need Rhonda guessing that he'd flipped through those pages more than a couple of dozen times in the last few years.

Great. Lee could see Rhonda working up to some kind of idiotic question by the way she gave her nose a double upward swipe.

"So ..." she said.

Yep, bring it on, sister, thought Lee, wondering if he was about to woof his cookies again.

"So, like, what did your old man do for a living and how'd he croa ..." Lee watched Rhonda hesitate. He'd give her credit— even *she* couldn't be that much of an insensitive schmuck. Rhonda looked down at her fingernails as if she'd found something intriguing there. "So, like, what I mean to say is ... how'd he, like ... pass out?"

Lee let his head drop and grabbed the roots of his hair. "It's pass *on*, ya brickhead." He would have laughed if he hadn't felt like barfing.

"Pass out, pass on, what*ever*," said Rhonda, "If you don't wanna tell me, just ..."

"Don't have a hairy fit," said Lee. Truth is, Lee liked talking about his father's profession. "He was a photographer, if you must know."

Rhonda gave Lee a sarcastic "wowzers!" look. "Photographer as in ... like ... *click-click-click* all day long?"

Lee could see she didn't have an appreciation for the finer things. "Hey," he said, "my dad was the best at what he did. He even won awards."

He could see she was still unimpressed—he guessed she'd wanted to hear him say something cool like "broncobuster" or "movie stuntman."

"Hey," he said, "there were times his job was really dangerous."

"Well, I guess *so*!" grinned Rhonda. "A sprained index finger can be a serious thing."

"Yeah, well, even *you* would think twice about photographing a wild grizzly in the bush. *And*," he added, "he had to have mega patience and super stamina for his job."

He waited for Rhonda to ask why, but of course ...

Sigh. "Yeah," continued Lee stubbornly, "there were times when he'd sit in a boat with his camera focused, waiting with steel nerves to catch a shot of a jumping fish. And if he didn't get the shot that day, he'd go back the next."

Lee didn't care that Rhonda looked like she could care less. He continued. "He once took a picture of a jumping marlin that was so spectacular, it ended up in *National Geographic*." Lee rubbed his queasy stomach under the blankets. "And later he totally got into video cameras—we have a stack of nutty home movies that reach the family room ceiling." As soon as he'd said it, he knew it was a mistake. Next week he'd come home to find Gertrude, who needed no begging, showing Rhonda footage of himself, starkers in the bathtub. Lee decided to zip his lips. Anyhow, it was none of her business how his dad died. She didn't need to know about the poor guy's blocked arteries. That part he wasn't fond of talking about.

"Still got his camera?" asked Rhonda. The question surprised Lee.

"And what if I did?"

Rhonda turned her back toward him. "Just wondered if you ever fiddled with it." Another swipe of the nose.

"Yeah, right," said Lee. "That'd be like some amateur picking up Elvis's guitar and forcing it to squawk."

"Hmm ..." said Rhonda. Lee didn't bother guessing the meaning of her tone. What did she know, anyway? Not much. And he meant to keep it that way.

Crap, thought Lee, next thing you know she'll be straining across my bed trying to read my wall. Sure as spit, right on cue,

Rhonda piped up with: "What are *those*?" pointing to the curling strips of paper held to his wall with masking tape.

Truth is, Lee was a closet quote-junkie—ever since the day he'd been searching the Web and clicked the pop-up "fart button" for a free download that invited him to *Climb inside the heads of the Famous, the Great, and the Successful!! Receive a new "SmartQuote" every day and GET SMART*. For Lee, it had been a no-brainer. Yeah! Why not pick the brains of the brilliant who have already test-driven life and figured it all out? He'd learned all about his computer by reading *PCS for Dummies*. A quote a day could very well be the equivalent to *Life's Secrets For Dumb-dumbs*.

For months now, he'd been receiving and memorizing quotes from the brilliant (and occasionally, not so brilliant). Things like:

Life is pretty simple: You do some stuff. Most fails. Some works. You do more of what works.
– Leonardo da Vinci

If you don't want your dog to have bad breath, do what I do: Pour a little Listerine in the toilet.
– Jay Leno

In the book of life, the answers aren't in the back.
– Charlie Brown

But it was the Albert Einstein gems that seemed to grab his attention the most, and he faithfully copied those down on scraps of paper whenever they appeared on his computer screen, and stuck them to the wall. 'Course, Lee had no desire to share them with Rhonda today (or *any* day), so he diverted her attention.

"Say, do you think you could pass me that ginger ale?"

She did, but resumed her snooping the minute the bottle left her fingers. Lee was getting more than a little peeved. Rhonda totally ignored him when he told her to put his baseball cap back where she'd found it, *please*—on the head of his life-sized cardboard cutout of Albert Einstein. Rhonda put it on her own head, instead. She turned the peak to the back, pulled up a wooden chair, and sat on it backwards. Resting her chin on the back of the chair, she took a good long look at Lee.

"Why do you do it?" she finally asked.

"What?"

"Knock yourself out over all this stuff. What's so important about bouncing a basketball twelve hours straight?"

Lee rolled his eyeballs again—*ouch!* He sighed.

"It's all about the zone," he mumbled, not expecting Rhonda, of all people, to understand. He could see her about to interrogate him so he cut her off. "You know, the *zone*?" (Like, duh … no harm in making her feel a bit dumb in the process.) "You enter the zone when you're concentrating so hard, the rest of the world doesn't exist. It's just you and the basketball. It's not you and your homework, or you and your crappy marks, or you and your boring, unexceptional existence. It's you, the ball, and the record you're trying to set." Lee tucked the sheet under his chin. "And besides," he said, wishing he had his zone back to himself again, "it gives me time to think."

Most of the time, he gave Rhonda only partial or guarded truths about himself—you couldn't be too careful with girls, he figured. But today, he didn't have the energy to pick and choose his words. "Makes the waiting easier."

"Waiting? For what?"

Lee remained silent.

"Come on," she said. He closed his eyes.

"For whatever it is I'm going to be good at one of these days." Lee lifted himself up on one elbow. "Rhonda, do you ever feel ... I don't know, a kind of *fire* blazing inside, like a crazy yearning-burning in your guts, or your heart?"

"Heartburn? Heck, yeah, I ate a bowl of Agnes's chili once and—"

"No," he said. He lay back on his pillow and looked at the ceiling. Nothing was ever easy with Rhonda. He tried a different route. "Did you know that Albert Einstein's teachers pretty much decided he was one-crayon-short-of-a-full-box when he was a kid?"

"Yeah, right."

"No, *really*. They labeled him a 'slow learner' and a 'daydreamer.' And he was crappy at sports, too."

"Yeah, so what about it?" said Rhonda.

"Do you think that as a kid he had any idea of how great he would be one day? Do you think it's possible that he felt his greatness burning away in his heart, even before he knew what it would be?"

For a second, Lee thought he caught a flash of something in Rhonda's eyes, as if she maybe understood what he was talking about all too well. But she looked away before he could read her. He flopped back down on his pillow. All he really wanted was sleep, but Rhonda was so crummy at taking a hint. He reached down and picked up the empty four-liter ice cream pail his mother had left on the floor beside his bed—"just in case."

"What are you doing?" asked Rhonda.

Lee held his head over the bucket and pretended to gag. Rhonda jumped up and hightailed it out of there. "I just remembered," she called on her way down the hall. "I have a guitar lesson in a minute. Sorry I can't stay."

Lee put the bucket down and closed his eyes. He opened them a second later when he heard the screen saver on his computer click in. Oh, brother. He watched the huge floating letters waltz across the screen in a never-ending parade: RON RONALDSON

ROCKS RON RONALDSON ROCKS RON RONALDSON ROCKS
RON RONALDSON ROCKS RON .

Lee sighed. He put his worn copy of *The Old Man and the
Sea* under his pillow and laid an arm across sleeping Santiago.
Before long, boy, dog, and Old Man were slipping in and out of
each other's dreams.

> *I love sleep. My life has the tendency to fall apart*
> *when I'm awake, you know?*
> — *Ernest Hemingway*

CHAPTER FOUR

Lee lay with his eyes closed in that delicious state he sometimes felt before coming back from a very deep sleep—he didn't know the time of year, day of the week, or hour of the day, nor even his own name, age, or social standing. He might have been an Einstein, or a single-cell amoeba, for all he knew. It didn't really matter. And as the facts slowly drifted back to him one at a time—my name is Lee, I'm not an amoeba (or an Einstein), it's summer, not winter—he'd end up trying to figure out the day of the week just by the quality of the air. Lee was convinced that each day of the week had its own specific smell, and if you trained yourself, you'd be able to tell the difference between a Sunday and a Thursday with no other device than your nose.

Without opening his eyes, he sniffed the air. Wednesday. Had to be. He sniffed again. Or maybe Friday? No, no, no, smelled more like a Sunday. For sure, Sunday. *SUNDAY?!!!!!* Shoot! Lee threw off the covers and swung his feet to the floor. Sunday. Father's Day! His feet hit the empty bucket beside his bed (thankfully, it had remained empty all night) and he reached down and grabbed it on his way out. He tiptoed quickly to the kitchen—no point in waking Agnes; she'd only fuss over him and force him to eat a banana or something—opened the freezer, dumped a tray of ice cubes into the bucket, topped it up with cold water, then rummaged around in Agnes's cupboards for as many clean sponges as he could find. Father's Day. That meant only one thing to Lee—the day of the Manitoba Marathon.

Lee looked at the clock on the oven: 7:16 AM. The first runners would be appearing at the end of his street any minute now as they passed the eight kilometer mark. The blue lines marking the official marathon route had been painted down the middle of Harrow Street three days earlier. Every year, the appearance of those blue lines made him happy he didn't live anywhere else. By now, traffic would be blocked off and rerouted, the pavement just waiting for the pounding of thousands of rubber-soled feet. Lee ran to the front door, threw his running shoes on without bothering to stick his heels in or lace up, and scuffed out the door. Half a millisecond later, he rushed back into the house, paused before a picture of a fish on the living room wall, and said to himself (he wasn't partial to saying these kinds of things out loud), "Happy Father's Day, Frankindad." Satisfied, he ran back outside.

As he hurried down the sidewalk, the ice water from the bucket sloshed over the side and wet his legs, but Lee didn't notice. Four or five of his neighbors were already sitting in lawn chairs down by the stop sign, sipping from thermal coffee mugs, one reading the morning paper.

"Anything yet?" he asked, out of breath.

"Lead runners should be by any minute," said Mr. De Lucca, adjusting the earplug to his transistor radio. "Thought you were gonna miss it, for a second there."

"You know me better than that, Mr. D.," said Lee. He sat down on the curb and dumped the sponges into the cold water. He shaded his eyes with his hand and strained to see if there was any action happening a few blocks up. Nothing.

Mr. De Lucca watched Lee with an amused smile. "How come you don't ever run yourself, kid?" he asked.

"Asthma."

"Mmm, tough break," said Mr. D. "Those sponges good and cold?"

But Lee didn't answer. He saw the hint of a red flash in the distance. It would be the police escort driving a few meters ahead of the lead runners. Good. Lee dropped to the grassy boulevard and did a couple of push-ups (well, *one* push-up—he had about as much strength in his skinny arms as a stick-man with pneumonia) and some jumping jacks on the spot. Lee liked to feel his own heart pounding right along with the runners' when they passed by.

"Get your butt out of the chair, Mr. D., they're on their way."

Old Man D. struggled to get out of the lawn chair and Lee ran over and pulled him up by the hand. Mr. Skin 'n' Bones De Lucca just about came rocketing out of his seat—"Whoa, little dogie!"

"Oops, sorry," said Lee. He made sure Mr. De Lucca was steady on his feet before running back to the curbside. The others were putting their coffee mugs and newspapers down and ambling over to join him.

"There's a fella come all the way from Kenya for this one," said Mr. Penner. "They say he's likely to win. Ran two hours, forty minutes in his last marathon."

Lee could see them coming now. He wondered if it was just his imagination or if the sun was actually glinting off their sweat-drenched bodies like the twinkles on a sun-lit diamond.

As the police car drove slowly by, Lee felt an emotional lump rise in his throat (which made him feel like a total idiot). *What, am I turning into Agnes or something?* He gave a deep cough and pulled it together as the first runner came toward him with a look of powerful concentration. Lee liked to think he knew exactly what this guy was feeling.

"If he keeps up that pace, he'll be dead by twenty kilometers," said Mr. D. It was true; the runner was coming at them at quite a clip. Impossible to keep up that pace the whole forty-two kilometers. The curbside crowd began to clap and shout words of encouragement.

"Way to go, buddy!"

"Keep it up!"

"Only thirty-four kilometers to go!" shouted Mr. Dickson. His wife gave him a jab in the ribs.

Lee held up a dripping sponge. "Water?" he called. The runner put up his hand without stopping and caught the cold sponge in midair. He squeezed the water over his bald head, which looked like it could just about fry an egg right now. The runner tossed the used sponge over his shoulder without a thank-you, but that didn't worry Lee. He counted to twelve before the next runner approached. His deep brown skin made Lee wonder if this was the man from Kenya.

"Thanks!" called the runner as he snagged a flying sponge on his way by. The next set of runners came in a clump of four. Mr. D. had to help throw sponges. He looked as pumped as Lee to be connecting with these swift heroes, if only for a second. By the time all the sponges were gone, the runners were coming in droves, and Lee's throat was hoarse from all the hooting and hollering and "Way to go, man!"s.

Lee looked at his watch. The winner would be crossing the finish line at the university stadium in about two hours. Better get moving. "Agnes!" he hollered as he burst into the house, flinging the empty bucket on the counter. "I need bus fare. Do you have any?" Agnes slipper-shuffled out of her bedroom, gripping her housecoat close around her scrawny neck, squinting against the morning light. The first thing she did was put a hand to Lee's forehead.

"Bus fare?!" said Agnes. "Hate to tell you this, Sonny, but you're going nowhere today. You're not well, and—"

"I'm *fine!*" said Lee, raking through the spare change pot on Agnes's coffee table. "Honest, I've never felt better. Take a look at my tongue if you don't believe me!" Agnes insisted you could tell a multitude of things about a person's health just by reading their tongue. She was kind of weird that way.

"Put your tongue back in your mouth, Sonny," she said, fanning the air. "I wouldn't mind betting you haven't brushed your teeth today." Still, what she saw (or didn't see) on his tongue must have been enough to assure her that he'd recovered sufficiently from his sunstroke. She shooed him away from the money pot and sorted through it herself, until she came up with the right change.

"Where you going at this hour, anyway?" she asked, dumping a huge mess of coins in his hand—Agnes had a thing about using up all her pennies.

"Marathon," he said on his way out the door. "Tell Mom I'll be home after lunch! Thanks, Ag!"

As he rushed down the street, he could hear her yelling from the doorstep, "At least take a *banana* with you!"

Never mind a banana, Lee wished he could take *Santiago* along with him. Be nice to have a little company on such a day. He looked over his shoulder at Rhonda's house for a sec. Naa, he wasn't *that* desperate. He kept walking. Then slowed. Then stopped. Ah, what the heck. He turned around and jogged toward her house. He took the front steps three at a time and pounded on the front door. No response. The inside door was open, so he pressed his nose against the screen and looked in. He could see the sun glinting off Mr. Ronaldson's trophies lined up on the mantel—heavyweight boxer in his younger days. Lee was startled when a shadow passed over the trophies and he found himself staring at Mr. Ronaldson's wide chest.

Rhonda's dad opened the door, and Lee stepped inside. He was a little embarrassed to see that Mr. Ronaldson, holding an egg flipper, was wearing a pink gingham apron (which did nothing to tone down his look of annoyance). Mr. Ronaldson looked Lee over with an icy stare. Didn't say a word. Lee figured it was up to him. "Rhonda home?" he asked, throwing a couple of fake punches to break the ice. Didn't go over well. Lee thought Mr. Ronaldson might at least play along with the shadowboxing; maybe lift his own fists in a good-natured left-right. No way. The only thing Rhonda's father did lift was one eyebrow, and Lee could see that he was totally unimpressed. Disgusted. Downright *dangerous*, even. Just as Lee was wondering if Mr. Ronaldson might actually punch him a good one in the face *(maybe he's mad I caught him in Mrs. Ronaldson's apron?)*, the retired boxer broke out in a huge toothy grin and playfully roughhoused Lee to the ground.

"Had ya going there, didn't I?" he chuckled. Lee suddenly felt as frail as Mr. De Lucca against Mr. Ronaldson's massive bulk. Mr. Ronaldson laughed, and helped Lee up from the floor.

"Your mom ain't been feeding you the Wheaties or something, kid?" He turned then and called up the stairs, "Ron, *Bean*pole's here to see ya."

Great, thought Lee, another name to add to the ever-growing string. Lee, Sonny, Daddy, Beanpole McGillicuddy. Maybe he'd make it into the world book of records one day, after all.

When Mr. Ronaldson returned to the kitchen, Lee took a quick look around the cluttered entranceway. That'll do, he thought, as he pulled Rhonda's Blue Jays baseball cap from under a heap of shoes in the corner. He quickly stuffed it in his back pocket. Rhonda came clomping down the stairs in unlaced high-tops and very badly cut off cutoffs—one leg nearly reaching her knee, the other at least three inches shorter (did she do that on purpose, or *what?*)—and a T-shirt that said, *What are you lookin' at?* She was as uncombed and unkempt as ever, but with an added look of surprise—it wasn't every day that Lee showed up on her doorstep; in fact, it was only the second time in four years. The first time was with a measuring cup in hand—Agnes had run out of yeast on bread-making day (not that you'd ever know she put yeast in those homemade bricks she called bread). Rhonda checked Lee's hands. It appeared he was measuring-cup-less today. She gave her nose an upward swipe. "What's up, Daddy?"

Lee took her cap from his back pocket and handed it to her. "You left this at Agnes's the other day," he fibbed. "Thought you might be needing it."

"Oh … um, thanks," she said.

"Well," said Lee, halfway out the door, "I'd better run, or I'll miss my bus."

"Where you going?" she asked. By then he was halfway down the front steps.

"Marathon."

"*Hey*," she hollered after him, "can *I* go?"

Bingo, thought Lee. He faked a look of extreme hesitation. "Well," he droned, "I *guess* you can come. But hurry! And bring the right change for the bus!" Rhonda ran back in the house. "And comb your hair for a change, why don't ya?"

CHAPTER FIVE

Sunday, June 10

University of Manitoba

Pembina Highway—five kilometers short of

University Stadium

8:45 AM

Temp: 27 degrees Celsius

Humidity: High enough to make you wonder

if you showered in your clothes by mistake.

When Lee insisted on getting off the bus at the thirty-seven kilometer marker instead of five kilometers later at the finish line, Rhonda started to whine. "We've come all this way on a stinkin'" (here she shot a glare at the garlic lover sitting across from her), "sweaty old bus, and we're not even going to see them finish the race?!" Ever since he could remember, Lee had been at the finish line of the Manitoba Marathon with thousands of other onlookers, watching the runners fly across the finish line, victorious arms raised high in the air, and for sure, that had its own appeal. But seated comfortably in the stands of the university stadium, watching the runners enter the grounds and run their last loop around the asphalt track, already sure of their victory, already knowing they'd made it, was not what Lee had in mind this time.

"I'm looking for blood and guts this time," he said.

Rhonda stopped dead. "What are ya, some kind of a wacko sadist or somethin'?" She had to run to catch up to him.

"Maybe," said Lee, hurrying toward the crowds lining the street where the runners slogged by, "and maybe not."

As they squeezed their way through, Rhonda caught her first glimpse of what Lee meant by blood and guts. One of the runners on the far side of the road began to slow down to a walk, then stopped, bent over, and heaved, bringing up what seemed like gallons of water, probably everything she'd had to drink since the beginning of the race. Then, of all things, she wiped her mouth, took a deep breath, and kept on running. She *kept on* running. "That'd be it for me," said Rhonda. "You upchuck, you go straight to bed, where I come from. This is stupid."

Several other runners went past, looking exhausted but still in one piece. Others stumbled as they passed, clearly using every ounce of energy to take just one more step, and then another.

"Look at that," said Lee, pointing to one man who had obviously pulled a muscle along the way and was now wincing with every painful half-hop-half-limp. "Suffer like that, and you know you're alive," said Lee.

"Or half dead," muttered Rhonda. Lee took a sideways glance at her. He could see she was uncomfortable, as if, for her, witnessing people with their pain showing was too much like seeing them run by in their underwear. Like it was none of her business, and she wanted no part of it. Lee knew it was his business, though. He craved the intensity, the rawness of it all, and if that made him a wacko sadist, so be it. He liked to think that his own blood and guts would be put to the test one day and that, like these aching, sweating winners flying and limping past him, he'd pass with flying colors. No c-minuses then. A-plus, all the way. If that day ever came.

"Oh, man," said Rhonda, looking through her fingers at a runner coming straight toward them. Well, "straight" wouldn't exactly be the word. The young muscular guy was weaving and meandering like a drunk on a bender. His long wavy hair hung in his eyes, but Lee could see that this guy didn't need his sense of sight any more—he was running purely on instinct. When he stumbled onto the boulevard and just about knocked Rhonda over, she clung to Lee's arm as if only he could save her. Then she realized how it looked and shoved his arm away as if it were Lee, not she, who had placed her hand on his skinny arm. Lee was already too busy being irritated to be irritated. Some bozo on a bike rode slowly along the sidelines, yelling stupid things at the delirious runner, like, *"You can* *do it, you're looking great, you're looking* great!*" The poor guy *wasn't* looking great, not by a long shot, and Lee wanted to slap that biker's trap shut with a wide piece of duct tape.

As the runner passed them, Lee could hear him mumbling something half-familiar. Holy Ronald McDonald, thought Lee, when he recognized the runner's slurred chant: *"Two all-beef patties, special sauce, lettuce, cheese, pickles, onions, on a sesame seed bum."*

He turned to Rhonda. "The guy's starving. He needs something to eat." For the first time in his life, Lee wished he'd listened to Agnes and brought along a bleepin' banana. He grabbed Rhonda's sleeve. "You got anything on you?"

Rhonda's hand went protectively to her back pocket and she shook her head. "Nope."

"Come on," said Lee, "this is important—what've you got?"

"It's a Mars Bar, if you must know," said Rhonda, "and you're not getting your hands on it."

Lee screwed up his eyes and gave her a piercing, "you greedy little scum" look.

Rhonda sighed and handed over the half-melted Mars Bar. "There goes my allowance," she moaned. Lee snatched it and ripped the wrapper with his teeth. He ran a few steps next to the delirious runner who hadn't given up the chant: *"… pickles onions on a sesame seed bum …"*

"It's *bun*, bro, not bum," whispered Lee into the runner's ear, hoping to save the guy some embarrassment. Gad, wasn't it bad enough that he was staggering around like a zombie after one too many martinis? Lee shoved the Mars Bar into the guy's limp hand. "Here. You need this, dude. Go on, eat it. It might give you the strength you need to finish."

Although Lee's asthma was already acting up, he stayed with the runner long enough to recognize a change in his chant. At first the words weren't clear, but with every step the runner's voice became stronger. "*I think I can, I think I can ...*"

Lee's face opened into a broad smile. "I *know* you can, buddy," he whispered.

Whether you think you can or think you can't—you are right.
– Henry Ford

CHAPTER SIX

"Put your tongue back in your head, Lee," said Gertrude. It was the second time in two days someone had told him that.

Lee had the habit of licking a spot just above the upper left corner of his lip whenever he was concentrating hard. And he was concentrating hard now. Gertrude stepped away from the frying pan and tried to take a peek at what he was writing. Lee covered the page with his hands. "Just homework," he said. Gertrude gave a disbelieving grunt and went back to frying eggs.

"Why are you up so early, anyway?" she asked over her shoulder.

"Project due," said Lee. "Have to use the school library." He looked at her to see if she'd swallowed that one. The teddy bears on her backside stared blankly at him. That was his mother all over—hard as nails in most respects, but crazy enough to wear a huge pink bathrobe covered in fuzzy pooh-bears.

Lee went back to practicing his mother's signature, copied from an old canceled check lying on the kitchen table. When he had it just right, he scrawled it at the bottom of the note he'd already printed:

Please excuse Lee from school today. He isn't well.
– Gertrude McGillicuddy

He'd get Rhonda (well, *bribe* Rhonda) to hand it in to his teacher this morning. Figured a Mars Bar would about do it. He folded the note carefully in half, and then into thirds (the way mothers are prone to do), and tucked it into his bathrobe pocket. Then he bolted down the fried eggs and toast that Gertrude set in front of him. "Thanks, Mom," he said, spraying toast crumbs, and he hurried to his bedroom, wiping the corners of his eggy mouth on his bathrobe sleeve.

Once inside, Lee locked his bedroom door, pulled a box out from under his bed, dumped the items on the floor and surveyed them: one baseball cap, four granola bars, three water bottles, full, one cap gun, one empty margarine container with a string through a hole near its rim, a baggie full of fruit-and-nut trail mix (he thought about picking out those disgusting little dried papaya chunks, then decided he could always feed them to Santiago along the way), five dog biscuits, one dog leash, one collapsible white metal pole from his pup tent, one digital watch, one asthma inhaler, one Mars Bar, and one banana.

Lee sighed now as he looked at the huge pile of stuff on the floor. He lifted an invisible microphone to his mouth. "Note to self," he said aloud. "Wear cargo pants with big pockets." He already had his T-shirt picked out. He would have liked one with a marathon number written across the chest but settled instead for his Theory of Relativity shirt: *E=mc squared*. Which reminded him! Lee pounced onto his bed and scanned the Einstein quotes scrawled on bits of paper in his messy handwriting. Last week he'd chosen: *Put your hand on a hot stove for a minute, and it seems like an hour. Sit with a pretty girl for an hour, and it seems like a minute. THAT'S relativity.* (Not that Lee had ever had the pleasure, or even the *hope* of sitting with a pretty girl—gorgeous Charlotte Bailey, maybe? In your dreams, Lee—but he liked the quote anyway.) The week before that—around the time of a killer math exam, he'd chosen: *Do not worry about your difficulties in Mathematics. I can assure you mine are still greater.* Of course Lee didn't believe this of Einstein for a second, but it gave him heart to think that maybe genius didn't have *everything* to do with brain cells.

Today Lee stood before his wall of quotes, rubbing his chin: "Lemme see …"—then—"Bingo!" He peeled one of the Albert quotes from the wall, jumped off his bed, and stuck it to the corner of Einstein's cardboard mouth. He stepped back and read the words: *Only one who devotes himself to a cause with his whole strength and soul can be a true master. For this reason, mastery demands all of a person.*

"Mastery." Lee liked the sound of that word. After repeating it a couple of times, his feet took charge and led him instinctively to the living room, where he paused in front of a framed photograph on the wall. He sighed with awe at the clarity and perfection of the blue marlin breaking the water's surface with pure grace—the arch of sparkling water droplets dancing over its head, the joyful freedom of the moment caught so expertly by his father's camera. Lee fingered the first-place ribbon stuck to the picture's glass. "Mastery," he whispered. Then he ran back to his room and dove into his closet in search of his cargo pants.

If you wanna catch a big fish, you need maniac desire and a truckload of stubborn determination. You'll be sitting in your boat with your focused camera glued to your face, waiting for a marlin to come bustin' out of the water—the sun dancin' on her slick skin, drops of water flying like diamonds. Can't even take the time to shoo a skeeter from the end of your nose—sure as shootin', that's when she'll come leapin' out of the water and you've missed her. Come the fourth or fifth hour of waiting, you start to kinda wonder if you're nuts. You're not, though, and I've got the picture to prove it!

– Frankindaddy McGillicuddy

CHAPTER SEVEN

> Twenty years from now you will be more
> disappointed by the things that you didn't do
> than by the ones you did do. So throw off the
> bowlines. Sail away from the safe harbor.
> Catch the trade winds in your sails.
> Explore. Dream. Discover.
>
> – Mark Twain

"So what'll you give me if I do it?" asked Rhonda, snatching the folded note to Lee's teacher from his hand. Lee pulled the Mars Bar from one of his overstuffed pockets. Rhonda narrowed her eyes. "What are you up to?" she asked, "and what's *that*?" She was pointing to the margarine container hanging from his belt on a string.

Lee waved the candy bar in front of her face. "No questions. Either do it or don't. What'll it be?" Rhonda shook her head and grabbed the bar from his hand. Lee let the screen door slam and took off down Rhonda's front steps.

He whistled for Santiago, who leapt over the fence and

joined Lee, a frenzied blur of flying slobber, lunatic tail whacking, and over-excited piddling. Santiago always seemed able to sense a good adventure when it was about to happen. "Calm down, girl," said Lee, struggling to get the leash attached to Santiago's collar. "You're going to have to be calm if you expect anyone to believe you're a real seeing-eye dog; try for a little *dig*nity, cryin' out loud." Lee took the white collapsible tent pole from a side pocket and extended it. He put on his dark glasses. Then he tapped his white stick on the pavement in front of him all the way to the bus stop. It was the only way he could think to get Santiago onto a city bus.

When the bus finally arrived and the doors opened, Santiago went berserk with excitement; clearly she didn't understand the meaning of "dignity." Lee looked somewhere above the bus driver's head and said, "This the number 29?"

The driver stifled a laugh and said, "Get on, kid."

Lee made an elaborate show of trying to feel his way to the fare box. The bus driver held up a transfer and said, "Need this?"

"Yeah, thanks," said Lee, making a grab for it, but she wouldn't let go.

"Caught ya!" she sang.

"Shoot." Lee took off his glasses. "This mean we have to get off?"

"Sit down, kid. I give you an A-plus for originality. So happens

I like a kid with some spunk." Lee sank into a seat. He supposed he should be thankful. It was the one and only A-plus he'd ever received in his life.

"What's the mutt's name?" asked the driver.

"Santiago."

"*Old Man and the Sea*?"

Lee's mouth dropped. "You're the first person who ever figured that out. How'd you *know*?"

"Fell in love with Hemingway as a teen," she said with a wink and a grin. "Where you headed?"

"University."

"That so?" The bus driver looked hard at Lee, then back at the road. "You one of those child geniuses going for his PhD at the age of eleven?"

"I'm thir*teen*," muttered Lee, insulted.

The driver came to a stop and opened the doors. Lee wondered if she was about to tell him to get off. Instead, an old man got on and clomped heavily up the steps.

"Yer six and a half minutes late," he barked at the driver. The guy was dripping with crankiness—and other things as well. He wiped his drippy nose on the back of his hand. Then he waved a crumpled bus schedule two inches from the driver's nose. "It says right here in black and white that you were supposed to be here six and a ha—"

He never did finish the sentence. Santiago, who must have smelled the ten-day-old hamburger grease on the guy's pants leaped up for a harmless sniff. The guy went ballistic. "What the … This here's public *transit*, lady," he yelled at the driver, "and that there's a *mutt*, in case you didn't notice." He clutched his leg. "Dang ugly thing took a chunk outta my leg …"

Lee was about to defend Santiago—not only was she nowhere *near* ugly—any old fool could see that—but she wouldn't bite a flea, even if it was dancing on her butt, that's how gentle she was. The bus driver saved him the trouble. "Sir!" she said to the geezer, "have you no re*spect*?!"—she pretty much spat the word at him—"The 'mutt' to which you refer is a *seeing-eye* dog," she said, "and this young man happens to be blind." Lee slipped his dark glasses back on.

"Not only that," continued the driver, "but the lad is only ten years of age and already working on a PhD in …" she looked at Lee's *E=mc squared* T-shirt, "… in Quantum Physics at the University of Manitoba." *Thir*teen! Lee wanted to interject, but resisted. "Now, if you'd move to the back of the bus, I'd be obliged. You're in the 'Special Needs' section and I'm quite sure,"—she eyed the old crankpot icily—"that there is very little *special* about you, sir." Lee loved her instantly.

They chatted all the way to the university, while Mr. Crotchety Pants fumed and cussed in the back seat. When Lee rang the bell to get off the bus, the driver said, "What's your name, kid?"

"Lee," he said, "Lee Sonny Daddy Beanpole McGillicuddy."

"It was a pleasure, Beanpole," she said. Lee turned around on the bottom step. "Hey, what's yours?"

"Ernestine," she said, "Ernestine Martha Margaret Mary Heming."

"The pleasure was all mine, Ernestine," said Lee. Santiago seconded it.

Lee got out his tent pole and tapped his way down the sidewalk for the benefit of the old grump glaring from the back window of the number 29 bus. As he passed a sunny storefront, he caught a glimpse of his reflection in the window as if projected onto a movie screen. Oh yeah, Lee often found himself standing on the outside of his life looking in—as if the scenes he saw flashing by made up some low-budget B movie with himself as the main actor. Half the time he wasn't even sure if he was starring in a tragedy or comedy. He only knew there were days when he could just about hear the stage director's voice booming from a bullhorn:

LEE'S CRAPPY LIFE: TAKE 334

CAMERA THREE, LET'S GET A CLOSE-UP OF THE KID LOOKING INTO THE STORE WINDOW. SOMEONE MOVE HIS WHITE CANE SO IT'S MORE VISIBLE. AND STOP

THE MUTT FROM TAKIN' A LEAK AGAINST THE BUILDING, FER CRYIN' OUT ...

Lee took a look at his reflection in the store window and shook his head. Comedy. Definitely. Am I loony-toons or *what*?

> *A question that sometimes drives me hazy:*
> *am I or are the others crazy?*
> *– Albert Einstein*

CAMERAS FADE

AAAAND, CUT!

CHAPTER EIGHT

{
**There was never yet an uninteresting life.
Such a thing is an impossibility. Inside of the
dullest exterior there is a drama, a comedy,
and a tragedy.**
– Mark Twain
}

MCGILLICUDDY HOUSE INTERIOR

10:17 AM

ROLL CAMERAS

Gertrude McGillicuddy ran her red lipstick across her mouth, and pressed her lips together in front of the mirror. She was more than satisfied with the way she looked. Not everyone could weigh a hundred and ninety-five pounds and come off looking so ... what, regal? impressive? elegantly monumental? All of the above, decided Gertrude, who considered herself a white Queen Latifah, of sorts. She sucked in her tummy and admired her reflection. Gertie knew she could have been a star if she'd wanted. Fact is, she *was* a star, in a way.

She tied her red neckerchief in a knot, donned her cowboy hat, and left the house. It wasn't her day to work at the Country and Western Club, but she was headed in that direction anyway.

"Hey!" she hollered as she burst through the front doors, letting a shaft of sunlight sneak into the dimly lit bar. She stood in the doorway, grandly silhouetted for a second. Gertrude was partial to big entrances.

Voices came at her from every direction, rising above the twangy strains of country and western pouring from the jukebox.

"Hey, Gertie!"

"Good to see you, Gert!"

"Thought it was your day off, Trude!" (Gertrude had almost as many names as her son.)

"Does a gal have to be working to enjoy the company of her friends?" she said. Gertrude playfully tipped a cowboy's hat over his eyes as she passed by, swiped someone else's beer bottle and pretended to guzzle it, handing it back with a belch that had them wondering if the bottle really was empty. Someone affectionately threw a balled-up napkin at her, and she took the smiling culprit by the collar and faked a punch to his gut. Everybody laughed. Although it was her job to play the heavy and keep peace in the club when things got a little too rowdy, and even though it had been necessary over the years to show more than a few people the door, that didn't stop them from loving Gert. Everyone did.

That's just the way it was.

"Joe!" she said, walking over to the bar. No matter how many years she'd worked there, Gertrude never tired of the sound of peanut shells crunching between her cowboy boots and the hardwood floor. "How's it going, my friend?" she said.

The bartender smiled back. "You first," he said. "How's life treating *you*, Gert?" Joe knew that when Gertrude came to sit at his bar on her day off, it usually meant she had something on her mind. Listening was as much a part of his job as pouring drinks.

"The usual?" he asked.

Gertrude nodded. "Better make 'er a double."

"One double swamp water comin' up," he said, lifting a glass first to the Coke fountain, then the Seven Up, then the Orange Crush. Gertrude didn't drink alcohol, but she was a woman who fiercely enjoyed her swamp water.

"A double, eh?" said Joe, taking a closer look at her. "What's up?"

Gertrude looked back at him, silent for a second, then she spoke. "Joe, you have a boy or two at home, right?"

"Four," said Joe.

"Any of them young teenagers?"

"Yep."

Gertrude took a slug of her soda. "Any of them give you trouble?"

"Gertie, I'll ask you again," said Joe, with a patient smile. "What's up?"

Gertrude sighed. "Paid a visit to the school earlier. Lee forgot his lunch so I dropped it off for him." She looked up at Joe. "He wasn't there."

"Hmm," said Joe.

"Forged my name on a sick note," she said.

"Oooh, boy," cringed Joe.

"I don't know, Joe," said Gertrude. She took a peanut from a basket, cracked it, and tossed the empty shell onto the floor (shell-tossing was compulsory at the Country and Western). "He's a good kid. A *really* good kid, but sometimes I worry about him. He seems happy enough most of the time, I suppose, but he hangs around by himself too much. Boy of his age should be out with his buddies. I'd almost be happy if I thought he'd skipped school today if it was to be with some other flesh-and-blood kids. It'd make a nice change from hangin' with his dead buddies all the time."

Joe furrowed his brows at Gertrude. "Come again?"

Gertrude smiled. "Don't worry. It's just that he's constantly memorizing quotes from people long dead and gone." Gertrude took a slug of swamp water, leaving a red lipstick kiss on the rim of her glass. "Mind, I suppose he does come up with some wise sayings, but it's unnatural for a kid his age, you ask me."

"Does Lee have any other hobbies to keep himself occupied?" asked Joe.

"That's the problem," she sighed.

CUT TO UNIVERSITY OF MANITOBA CAMPUS

9:18 AM

ZOOM IN ON FIGURE OF BOY AND DOG WALKING

Without ambition one starts nothing. Without work one finishes nothing. The prize will not be sent to you. You have to win it.
– Ralph Waldo Emerson

Lee looked around the campus at the hustle and bustle of hardworking (judging by the stacks of books they were lugging) summer students rushing from building to building. Made him think he could easily take up people-watching as a hobby. They were different in so many ways from one another, yet they all had that *student* look on their faces. They seemed to have a purpose, and to know exactly what it was, and for that reason, it was more than a little bizarre that he felt as if he fit in perfectly. But purpose was seeping from his very pores this morning.

Lee untied the margarine container from his belt, put it on the ground, and filled it with water from one of his bottles.

"Have a good long drink," he said to Santiago. "You're in for a workout." Lee took a swig from the bottle himself, put it back in one pocket, and pulled his cap gun from the other. They were standing outside the Max Bell Sports Center at the very spot where thousands of runners had only yesterday crammed in at the starting line of the Manitoba Marathon. Lee was a day late, and he'd be walking the course instead of running, but right now that mattered little to Lee. When Santiago was finished drinking, Lee tied the margarine container back onto his belt. He set his digital watch, raised the cap gun / starting pistol above his head, and looked down at his dog. "Ready, girl?"

CUT BACK TO JOE'S BAR

ZOOM IN ON GERTRUDE'S FINGERS CRACKING PEANUTS

"Thing is, the kid's *nuts* about setting his own records," said Gertrude to Joe. "Obsessive, almost. When he was eight, he saved his allowance for months so he could buy enough dominoes to set up the length of a full city block."

"Dominoes?"

"*You* know," said Gertrude, "the way they line 'em up and then set the whole thing in motion with a nudge."

"A full city block," whistled Joe. "That must have been impressive."

"Not really," said Gertrude. "He'd get just so far before a chipmunk or a neighborhood cat would come along and knock a domino over, and then, well, you know. He must have started over fifteen times before he finally gave up and moved the whole shebang into the house. I was tiptoeing for days."

"Sounds like a kid with determination," said Joe, "and that's a good thing, don't you think, Gertie?"

"Determination and patience he has by the truckload," said Gertrude, "but it seems to me he could get more bang for his buck if he'd invest it in something a little more important than dominoes. Ah, shoot," sighed Gertrude.

CUT TO UNIVERSITY CAMPUS

CATCH SUN GLINTING OFF BARREL OF CAP GUN

ROLL SOUND

BANG! Lee's cap gun fired, and an insanely startled Santiago took off faster than a bullet. Even though Lee intended to walk the marathon, he was forced to run the first fifty meters. "Hold your horses, Santi," he panted, afraid the leash would pull his arm right out of its socket. "It was just a starting gun. Haven't you ever heard of a starting gun?"

CUT TO JOE'S BAR

"Haven't you ever heard of passion?" said Joe to Gertrude. "Sounds to me like the kid's got it in spades. And that's gotta come in mighty handy one day when he finds out where his talents lie. He'll probably grow up to be a van Gogh, or an Einstein, or something."

"Maybe you're right," said Gertrude, downing her glass and standing up.

"Now don't be too hard on him," said Joe. "You going out looking for him?"

"Hell, no," said Gertrude. "I'm certain he's not up to anything dangerous. He's got a good head on his shoulders." She scooped up a handful of peanuts from the bar for the road. "It was the marathon yesterday. That always seems to fan his fire." She smiled at Joe. "Or should I say, his *passion*. If I know Lee, he's probably gone out to run forty-two kilometers backwards on a pogo stick or some crazy thing." She lifted her hat. "Thanks for the wise words, Joe. You're a prince among bartenders."

FADE TO A HEADSHOT OF LEE, TALKING INTO INVISIBLE MICROPHONE

"Note to self: Next year, think about training to be the first person to walk the marathon backwards." Lee looked down at Santiago, who had calmed down enough by now to enjoy the walk. "If I did that," he said to Santi, "you really *could* be my seeing-eye dog."

CHAPTER NINE

{
Some men give up their designs when
they have almost reached the goal,
while others, on the contrary, obtain
a victory by exerting, at the last moment,
more vigorous efforts than ever before.

– Herodotus
}

By thirty-seven kilometers, Lee was going through his predictable "Am I nuts?" phase. If his life *was* some kind of crappy movie, it definitely wasn't a comedy anymore. He slowed down, bent over, and took Santiago's jowls in his hands. He looked her straight in the eyes. "Am I nuts, girl? What are we doing? Why are we *doing* this, Santi?"

Santiago licked Lee's face and gave a questioning whine. Lee sighed, glanced at his watch, and kept walking. Seven and a quarter hours they'd been trudging. His "bring-it-*on*-bro" enthusiasm had left him at sixteen kilometers. It hit him hard when he realized that, aside from the red spot on his white ankle sock from a busted blister, there'd be no blood and guts for him here today. It's only the sweating, give-it-all-you've-got runners who hit that heart-breaking, soul-sucking "wall," thought Lee. Walkers? Oh yeah, they ache, they hurt, but they'll never have the kind of agony *or* the ecstasy of a true hero.

Instead of bricks, Lee imagined his "wall" made of a thin, unbreakable membrane—strong enough to bounce him back every time he tried to break through, but thin enough (like the over-stretched wall of a chewing gum bubble) to be able to see vague shadows of something better on the other side.

"What the heck are we doing, Santi?"

As if in answer, Santiago stopped to take a whiz near an apparently interesting-smelling tree. Lee sat on the curb. He tried to remember the word that had leapt out at him from this morning's Einstein quote, the one he'd read when he was still chipper and undaunted and certain that he was not a nutcase. What was it, anyway? Something about … oh yeah, *Mastery*.

Lee absentmindedly pulled up his sock, which unfortunately took the stuck-on top of his weepy blister along with it. *Shoot.* He wondered if he'd ever really be "master" material at anything, or (and this felt much more likely) remain forever "mediocre." Mediocre at everything.

Mastery. Mediocrity. What's it gonna be, Lee?

He tossed Santiago a dried passion fruit from his trail mix. "Know what Einstein said, Santi?" He took her yip as a yes. "Only one who devotes himself to a cause with his whole strength and soul can be a true master … mastery demands *all* of a person."

Einstein, thought Lee, I sure hope to heck you know what you're talking about. "Okay then, girl," he said, "Time to give it our all."

As they passed the thirty-seven kilometer marker, Lee began a slow jog. Santiago, for her part, was ecstatic. She galloped ahead until the leash was taut and soon she had him picking up speed. Lee suddenly remembered why he'd decided to walk this marathon instead of running it. He could feel his lungs protesting. He was about to tell Santiago to give him a break, to "slow *down*, ya maniac, you've obviously never suffered with asthma," but when he opened his mouth, something entirely different flew out: "Frig it." Lee was suddenly overtaken by an overwhelming urge to let the pain grow and intensify until he exploded into a million mediocre bits, blowing through his mediocre universe. He caught up with Santiago and started running at a punishing speed. The more it hurt, the faster he ran. His heart became a pair of boxing gloves, pounding the inside of his chest: left-*right*, left-*right*—thump-*thump*. He could even feel the pounding in his temples, like the top of his head was about to blow off. Yep, here it comes. Self-combustion. Lee McGillicuddy up in smoke. POOF! Nothing left but a smoldering heap of cinders. He was waiting for it, expecting it. But it didn't come.

Instead came the miraculous: Without warning, without explanation ... jeez ... he started to feel good. Absurdly, ridiculously good. And *strong*. Strong enough to spin the planet on the tip of his finger like a basketball. And then he did it— the impossible. He maxed his speed, screwed his eyes shut, spread his arms wide, and took a suicidal leap at his "wall"— that rubbery membrane of mediocrity that stood between him and mastery—and instead of rebounding into space ... holy crud ... HE ... BROKE ... *THROUGH*. As Lee stepped onto the track at the university stadium—the same track that thousands of marathoners had stepped onto only yesterday as they took their last steps toward the finish line—he knew he'd broken through.

It was like putting on perfect prescription glasses when you didn't even know your eyesight was crappy. It was like having a huge plug of wax removed from an ear that you didn't know had been blocked up for years. The volume was up and everything seemed vibrant and sharp and full of possibility. He'd done it. Lee Sonny Daddy Beanpole McGillicuddy, if only for a tiny, infinitesimal fraction of his life, had entered Mastery.

Only those who will risk going too far can possibly
find out how far one can go.
– T. S. Eliot

You can become a winner only if you are willing to walk over the edge.

– Damon Runyon

CHAPTER TEN

Slang Kischuk looked up from his soccer practice inside the university stadium and did a double take. He saw a boy and a dog coming through the gates onto the track. The dog was bounding, and the kid had his arms raised high in the air. He was running sideways, facing the empty stands as if they held thousands of cheering fans. He was staggering; Slang could see he was exhausted, but the kid nodded toward the stands and croaked, "Thank you! Thank you very much." Must be hallucinating, thought Slang—unfortunately he knew a thing or two about "Hallucination City" from recent personal experience. (Slang cringed at the sudden memory of a talking sesame seed bum.)

"Kischuk!" yelled the coach. "We don't have time for daydreaming here. Get with the program or get off the field!"

But Coach Thorwaldson lost the attention of more than one of his players as they stopped to stare at the strange spectacle coming around the track.

"Someone should tell that kid the marathon was yesterday," joked one of them.

"Maybe he's been running *since* yesterday," called another.

"Maybe he's going for a world record." He held an invisible microphone in front of a teammate's face: "Tell me, son, how does it feel to hold the world record for the slowest marathon ever run?" Some of them laughed. But Slang was too fresh from his own marathon experience to find it funny—he still had the aching muscles to remind him. He began walking toward the boy and his dog, and a small crowd followed. The coach blew a sigh of frustration, but his curiosity was as strong as anyone's. He trailed behind them.

Slang reached the finish line just in time to catch Lee as his knees gave way. He took Lee by the armpits and laid him out on the track. The kid was mumbling, trying to say something.

"What?" said Slang, lowering his ear.

"Puffer," choked Lee. "Left pocket."

Slang dug around in Lee's pocket until he found his asthma inhaler. He put it to Lee's lips and pressed the nozzle. It took a few minutes, but Lee started to breathe easily again, and the whole time the smile never left his face. "*I broke through,*" he whispered.

Far better is it to dare mighty things … than to rank with those poor spirits who neither enjoy much nor suffer much, because they live in a gray twilight that knows not victory nor defeat.

– Theodore Roosevelt

CHAPTER ELEVEN

{
**Be not forgetful to entertain strangers
for thereby some have entertained
angels unawares.**

– Hebrews 13:2
}

"Take him up to his front door and make sure his parents are home, Kischuk," called Coach, as Slang helped Lee toward the parking lot. "And make sure you show up for the game good and early tomorrow!"

The coach, being a devoted dog lover *and* the devoted husband of a woman with dog allergies, roughhoused with Santiago another second or two before reluctantly letting her go. "Beauty," he whispered as she loped off to catch up with Lee.

"You didn't have to volunteer to take me home," said Lee on the way to Slang's car. "Really, we don't mind taking the bus."

"Are you kidding?" said Slang, "you're my ticket outta here today, kid." He grimaced from the pain in his calves. "No person should be subjected to a soccer practice the day after running a forty-two-kilometer marathon." He playfully elbowed Lee.

"Consider yourself my angel of mercy."

Never mind an angel, Lee felt like a pipsqueak beside this muscular athlete. Even so, he realized with some pride that he also felt a certain kinship. After all, they'd both recently experienced "the agony and the ecstasy" firsthand, right?

Slang unlocked the car door for Lee. "Ignore the mess," he said, clearing a pile of books and hamburger wrappers from the front seat. "Now, you're sure you're okay? I don't mind taking you to emerg," he said. "Asthma's a serious thing. I had it myself as a kid."

An*other* similarity, thought Lee.

"Never been better," said Lee, putting on his seatbelt, and he meant it. He reached an arm over to calm Santiago in the back seat. Lee wasn't exactly great at small talk, but at least there was the marathon. "So ... how'd you do in the race yesterday?"

"Pretty good in the first half," said Slang, who seemed so comfortable inside his own skin that Lee wondered if he'd ever suffered an awkward moment in his life. "But I ran into a little difficulty near the end." Lee couldn't imagine this guy having difficulty with *any*thing. Slang took the sweatband from his forehead and tossed it in the back seat. As he shook his wild hair loose, Lee had a feeling he'd met this guy somewhere before.

"Yeah," continued Slang, "it got kind of surreal there for a while. I started getting tired and crazy-*hungry*, and at thirty-seven kilometers I had a major meltdown." He looked over at Lee. "Keep that to yourself, though, eh kid? I've got a rep to maintain, if ya know what I mean." Slang chuckled. "Honestly. I thought I was gonna die." He glanced over at Lee, who had the amazed face of someone putting two and two together. Slang must have seen the stunned disbelief on Lee's face. "Really!" insisted Slang. "Got all delirious and everything. Thank God some guy on the sidelines stuffed a candy bar in my hand." Slang shook his head. "I don't think I'd have finished without it."

Lee was *bursting* to yell out, "It was *me*!! I was the guy who gave you the Mars Bar!! *I'm* the one who helped you finish the race!" He could barely stop himself from leaping about like Santiago did when she was happy.

Instead he checked his instinct to blabber like an excited six-year-old. He smiled to himself and said, as cool as he could, "Run into any sesame seed bums lately?"

"Huh?" said Slang.

"You know," said Lee, "two all-beef patties, special sauce ..."

Slang pulled the car to the curb and stopped. He looked at Lee in amazement. "No way!" Lee just smiled back at him. "No *way*!" repeated Slang. "You're the magic candy man?!"

In answer, Lee gave what he hoped was a mature smile.

"No way!" said Slang. "You saved my *life*, dude! That chocolate gave me the last ounce of energy I needed!"

For half a nanosecond, Lee thought about mentioning Rhonda, considering it *was* her precious Mars Bar. Then he told himself to get over it and claimed one hundred percent of Slang's shining approval.

"It was nothing," insisted Lee.

"No, it was something," said Slang. "It was definitely something, and I owe you, my friend." He pulled the peak of Lee's baseball cap down over his eyes, and then he popped Lee on the shoulder a couple more times. "No *way*, man! That's perfect!"

As Slang pulled up to Lee's house twenty minutes later, he turned to Lee, who hoped there wasn't another playful punch coming. Instead, Slang bopped Lee on top of the head. Then he took off Lee's baseball cap and mussed up his hair. "Here's my number. So you'll be there, right?"

"Wouldn't miss it," said Lee, taking a scrap of scribbled numbers from Slang.

"Need me to pick you up?"

Lee could see his mom standing at the front screen door with her arms crossed. "No, I'll see you there. Can I bring Santiago?"

"'Course!" Then Slang spotted Lee's mom as well. "Hey, maybe I should come and talk to your mom or some—"

"See you tomorrow," said Lee, pulling Santiago from the car. He pretty much floated up his front steps and into the house. Not even the word "grounded" could bring him down.

i thank You God for most this amazing
day: for the leaping greenly spirits of trees
and a blue true dream of sky; and for everything
which is natural which is infinite which is yes
– e. e. cummings

CHAPTER TWELVE

{
There are only two ways to live your life.
One is as though nothing is a miracle.
The other is as though everything is a miracle.
– Albert Einstein
}

{
What a day, eh, Milhouse? The sun is out,
birds are singing, bees are trying to have sex
with them—as is my understanding ..."
– Bart Simpson
}

Lee was still high when he opened his eyes the next morning. He woke before his alarm and got out of bed just because he felt like it. That in itself was miracle enough. More than once his mother had been forced to pour cold water on his forehead or pop ice cubes down his pajamas to stir him from his catatonic sleep states.

This morning it wasn't necessary. Lee looked out his window and had to touch his eyes to make certain he wasn't actually wearing those prescription glasses he'd imagined yesterday. It was true. Everything seemed hyper-focused and double-dipped in Technicolor. He wondered if this is what it felt like to look through the eyes of a winner.

Lee grabbed a shirt from his closet and did up the buttons. *Buttons*, marveled Lee; *what a simple, yet ingenious invention.* He thought about the history of mankind, and wondered how many centuries they'd been forced to struggle along without buttons before some inspired genius came up with the idea. Eureka! And how many more centuries till some brilliant dude dreamed up "denim," he thought, pulling on his ragged and superbly comfortable jeans. *Mr. Blue-Jean, whoever you are, I salute you!* And then he started to do up his zipper, and, well, that whole concept just about blew his mind.

In the bathroom, he stopped to notice how the shade of toothpaste on his toothbrush matched the color of his shirt exactly. It nearly made him want to skip brushing his teeth and just carry around the toothbrush all day. *Look!* he'd say to people on the street, *My shirt is a perfect toothpaste blue.* Did you ever wonder who was exceptional enough to invent toothpaste? Did you ever wonder why the stuff doesn't taste like Tub 'n' Tile Cleaner? What other cleanser in the world tastes that good?

Jeez-Louise, thought Lee, *I'd better be careful not to run too many marathons; I'm starting to sound like some love-struck dope in a gag-me-with-two-fingers chick flick.* He didn't care, though.

Not even about the blister on his ankle that was starting to bleed again. Or about the fact that he had to shuffle down the stairs on his bum because his calves were aching so badly. Minor details.

Nothing could bring him down today. Not the fact that there were only two Cheerios left in the bottom of the cereal box. Not the big black mess he had to clean up after scraping his burnt toast (Gertrude considered herself a "Mrs. Fix It," but Lee could have told her to stay away from that malfunctioning toaster). Not even the fact that he had math today, and Mr. Wood would be handing their exams back. Shoot, that *exam*, thought Lee. Nope, nope, nope, he told himself a second later, not even a failing math mark could bring him down today.

"What did you burn?" asked Gertrude, fanning the air with her morning paper as she came into the kitchen.

"Hate to tell you, but the toaster worked better before you fixed it, Mom," said Lee. Then he pulled out a kitchen chair and motioned her to sit down. "Your breakfast is served, Madame." Lee plunked the plate of murdered toast in front of her.

"Are the planets spinning out of orbit or something?" said Gertrude. "Seems to me this is the second day in a row you've actually been up before me." She picked up a piece of toast and stared at it before taking a bite from the least burnt corner. As she chewed, she took an even closer look at Lee. "C'm'ere," she said. "You look different today."

"It's the shirt," said Lee. "Turns out toothpaste blue's my color."

"Huh?"

Lee thought this might be a good time to ask his mother about lifting his grounding so that he could go to Slang's play-off soccer game like he'd promised to. But somehow he felt that it wasn't necessary. On days like this, things had a way of falling into place naturally. He felt it in his bones.

Whoa! thought Lee, when his mother echoed his thoughts half a second later. "So, you say you promised this Slang character you'd go to his game tonight?"

"Before I knew I was grounded," said Lee.

"Well," said Gertrude (maybe it was his gesture of making her toast that had buttered her up), "I've always believed in honoring your promises." He looked at her. "And I suppose I'm grateful that he helped you home last night."

Lee smiled.

"But don't think I'm going soft, young man," she said. "Pull another stunt like that and you're grounded for life." Lee hugged his mother, who pretended not to like it. Lee loved her when she put on an act.

On his way to school, Lee knocked on Agnes's front door. He heard her shuffling to the door in her big crazy-cat slippers before he actually saw her. "Just wanted to say, 'Have a good day,'" he said, when she opened the door. "And hey, Aggie—"

"Aggie?!"

"—how about making some of your delicious banana bread soon? I've been dreaming about it lately!" Of course, he'd pay for this later when she put a piece of banana brick in front of him and expected him to eat it, but right now it seemed worth the look of surprised pleasure on her face. It took so little to cheer Agnes. He wondered why he didn't make a point of doing it more often. *Note to self ...*

After that, he stopped at Rhonda's.

"Beanpole!" said Mr. Ronaldson at the front door. Oh no, thought Lee. "Good to see you, kid," he said, wrestling Lee to the ground, then popping him up so fast Lee felt like a yo-yo.

Rhonda rolled her eyes and pushed her dad back to the kitchen, but not before Lee had a chance to see the words written on his apron: WORLD'S NUMBER ONE MOM.

"What do you want?" said Rhonda suspiciously, when she returned. "Got some more dirty work you need me to do? It's gonna cost you more than a Mars Bar this time."

Lee laughed. "Okay," he said, palms raised in the air, "I just came to see if you wanted to walk to school together, but ..." he started down her front steps, "hey, if you're not in the mood, that's cool."

He got halfway across her yard before Rhonda believed her

ears. She jumped into her high-tops, grabbed her backpack, and ran to catch up. "Wait up, ya idiot!" she called. That was about as useless as saying, "Wait up," to a helium balloon without a string. Lee had his own momentum today, and Rhonda could see that she'd just have to *keep* up. "What's your hurry, pea-brain?" Lee slowed down so she could catch up (another miracle!), then playfully bum-checked her onto the boulevard. "Hey! You combed your hair, for a change," he said. "Looks good."

Rhonda narrowed her eyes. "I had my annual *bath*," she said, mussing her hair with her fingers until it looked like a rat's nest again. "What's up with you, anyway?" she said. "You're acting weird."

"Me? Weird?"

"Yeah, and I don't like it. I prefer you when you're a jerk."

Good old Rhonda, thought Lee, taking a swig from his water bottle. He handed it to her. "Here, take a huge mouthful and don't swallow."

"What?!"

"We'll see who can hold it in the longest. Come on."

"*Me*? Take a swig from something that just touched *your* lips? You got some kind of brain-eating virus, or *what*?"

"Just wipe it off, Turkey Gizzard. I'll bet you won't last more than twenty seconds."

Rhonda grabbed the bottle and wiped it a couple of hundred

times on her T-shirt. Even then, she refused to let the bottle touch her lips. She put her head back and poured in a big mouthful. Lee took the bottle back and took his own huge swig. He already knew from experience that it doesn't take long to feel like a bozo-brain when your mouth is bulging with water, and what's left then but to laugh? Rhonda was the first to explode, spraying water everywhere, and choking with laughter. Lee lost it soon after that.

Rhonda tried several more times to outlast Lee but lost every time. They were getting soaked.

"Come on," said Rhonda. "One more time. I know I can do it."

Lee took an extra huge mouthful and looked up just in time to see—oh no, *please*, no—gorgeous Charlotte Bailey crossing the street toward him. Had she ever said a word to him in her entire life? Of course not. Did she choose today, when he was holding a gallon of water in his mouth like some dork, to acknowledge him? Of course. "Hi Lee."

Lee tried swallowing his water in one gulp—what was he going to do, hork it out in front of her?—but he took in some air as he swallowed, and the pain of it going down made his eyes water. He opened his mouth to say "Hi," but the word came out trapped inside a huge belch.

She looked at him, stunned for a second, then shook her

head and said one word: "Charming." As gorgeous Charlotte Bailey walked off, Rhonda fell on the sidewalk clutching her gut with laughter.

On any other day, this would have been enough to ruin Lee's day (his *year*). But, nope. Not today. Nope, nope, nope. I'm fine, thought Lee. Really, I'm *fine*. He looked down at Rhonda and yelled it out loud: *"I'm fine!"* which sent Rhonda into another wave of hysterics.

CHAPTER THIRTEEN

{ I ain't no physicist, but I knows what matters.

– Popeye the Sailor Man }

Doesn't matter, thought Lee. I'm no Einstein, but at least I know what matters and what doesn't, and this math mark *doesn't*. Said it before, and I'll say it again: Ain't nothin' gonna bring me down today.

When Mr. Wood entered the class, Lee McGillicuddy wasn't the only kid trying to convince himself that a failing math mark wasn't the end of the world. Decimals are no picnic, and judging by the look on Mr. Wood's face, the exam results were dismal.

"*People*," he said, rocking on his heels and tilting his head back to look at them through the bottom of his bifocals. "Either I'm the world's worst teacher, or you geniuses neglected to study. And I'd put my money on the latter. How about you?"

No one bothered to answer. Most of the students stared down at various names scratched on top of their desks. On his own desk, Lee zeroed in on a badly carved heart with the words *Charlotte Bailey Loves L.M.* engraved inside; clearly the work of some brainchild with a turds-for-brains sense of humor, thought Lee.

"Now, this was an important exam," continued Mr. Wood. "It counts for twenty percent of your final mark. And as you well know, there are no rewrites for final exams." He looked around at the glum faces currently avoiding his glare. "For those of you who weren't listening, as usual, I will repeat that last sentence,"—and here Mr. Wood raised his voice for the benefit of the habitual non-listeners—"THIS EXAM COUNTS FOR ..."

Few people in the class missed the undertones of someone's disgusted mumbling.

Mr. Wood certainly didn't.

"Mr. McGillicuddy!" he said, his words as sharp as a yardstick whacking a desktop. "It seems you have something important to say. Please say it loud enough for the benefit of all."

"That's okay," said Lee, reddening.

"It is *not* okay," said Mr. Wood. "It is not okay, at all. If your thoughts are important enough to interrupt my class, they must be of *utmost* significance, and I for one would not want to deprive the class of such momentous thoughts."

Lee remained silent, and then he thought, *Fine. You want to know, I'll tell you.* He stood up beside his desk and repeated what he had formerly mumbled. This time his words were loud and clear. "Not everything that *counts* can be *counted*, and not everything that can be counted *counts*."

Mr. Wood raised his eyebrows. "Well, Mr. McGillicuddy," he said, clasping his hands behind his back and looking down at the tips of his nerdy shoes, "if I were an English teacher, I would give you an A-plus for such inspired originality, but as it is, I am a *Math* teacher, and—"

"Those aren't my words," interrupted Lee.

"No doubt," smiled Mr. Wood. "Whose, pray tell, are they?"

"Albert Einstein's."

"*Really*," said Mr. Wood, smugly looking at the rest of the class, even though he was addressing Lee. "And have you managed to keep anything *else* that Mr. Einstein said in that head of yours?" Two seconds of silence.

Okay, you asked for it, thought Lee. "As a matter of fact, yes, Mr. Wood. May I write it on the board?"

"Please," said Mr. Wood, holding up a piece of chalk for Lee.

Lee wondered if he'd finally gone and lost his cotton-pickin' mind as he walked to the front of the room. Still, it was too late for that now. He took the piece of chalk and wrote one sentence on the board: *The only thing that interferes with my learning is my education.* Then he signed Albert Einstein's name and underlined it three times.

"Well, well," cooed Mr. Wood, "a real *rebel*, your Mr. Einstein. Is there anything else you'd like to share with us before

I send you to the office for disrupting my class?"

Lee wondered if anyone could see the smoke that was surely pouring from his own scarlet ears. "As a matter of fact, yes," said Lee, and he turned back to the board and wrote one last sentence, his hand shaking this time: *Great spirits have always encountered violent opposition from weak minds.* This time he underlined Albert's name four times.

"And do tell us, Mr. McGillicuddy," said Mr. Wood, again addressing the class instead of Lee, "into which category do *you* fall? That of a great spirit or a weak mind?"

Some of Lee's classmates laughed.

"Laugh if you like," said Lee, cursing the wobble in his voice. "But there were enough dummies who believed that Einstein had a weak mind."

"And how would you know that, I wonder?" asked Mr. Wood.

"He was refused by the first university he applied to," said Lee. "They said he didn't show enough *potential* as a student."

More nervous laughter from the class. Mr. Wood waited for the laughter to die before saying, "And your point *is*?"

I'm okay. For sure. I'm *fine*, thought Lee, as he replaced the chalk on the ledge and slowly walked toward the door.

"Way to *go*, Einstein," called someone from the back row. Lee knew instantly that from this day on, he'd never be known by any other name. Well, there were worse names. Einstein. He'd wear it with pride.

I'm fine. Really. Nothing can bring me down today.

That's what he told himself as he stepped out into the hall.

Keep away from people who try to belittle your ambitions.
Small people always do that, but the really great make
you feel that you, too, can become great.
– Mark Twain

CHAPTER FOURTEEN

"Well, *finally*," said Agnes, when Lee walked in the door that day. "We were starting to worry. Where have you been?"

Lee stared at the spectacle in Agnes's front room. She was on her knees in front of Rhonda, who was standing on the leather footstool in her unlaced high-tops, with her bare, skinny legs sticking out of … some weird *thing* she was wearing.

"What the heck is *that*?" said Lee.

Agnes spoke around the pins sticking out of her mouth. "It's a bed jacket," she said. "I'm just finishing the hem." With that, she stuck a pin through the fabric and Rhonda came alive.

"Ouch!"

"Oops, sorry, love."

Lee stared at Rhonda in the bizarre looking "jacket." It looked as if it was made out of a pink bedspread. The sleeves hung at least six inches past Rhonda's fingertips. "What the heck is a *bed* jacket?"

"You wear it when you're sitting up in bed reading, or knitting, or some such thing," said Agnes.

"You *knit*?!" said Lee to Rhonda.

"It's not for *me*, ya big dough-brain. You think I'd be caught dead in something like this?"

"So who's it for?"

"Some old dear in the seniors home," said Agnes. "I'll take it along on one of my visits. I'll know exactly who it's for once I meet her."

Lee smirked at Rhonda who glared back at him.

"You didn't tell me why you're late," said Agnes.

Lee slumped into a chair. "I was sitting on a park bench."

"For two hours?!" Agnes took a closer look at Lee. "You okay?" she said.

"Yeah, I'm okay. I'm fine. Really."

Agnes took the pins from her mouth, stuck them into the pincushion, and got to her feet slowly, pressing her hands against the small of her arthritic back.

"You look different today," said Agnes. It was the second time in one day someone had told him that.

"You're very pale. Come here and let me see your tongue."

"No, I'm fine, yeah, really, no, never been better," mumbled Lee all the way to his bedroom. Agnes and Rhonda looked at one another.

Rhonda shrugged. "He's been acting *weird* all day." She wiped her perspiring forehead. "Can I get out of this ugly thing now?"

Lee was relieved to find that Rhonda wasn't joining them

for dinner that night. During the meal, Agnes kept a suspicious eye on Lee. He knew she was dying to ask him what was up—he was way too quiet for her liking—but he just didn't have the energy to talk about it. Instead, he said: "Bass the putter, please." That usually got a smile out of her. Today she just raised an eyebrow and passed the butter with one of her "you're not fooling me" looks.

"Your mother tells me you're going to a football game tonight, Sonny."

"Soccer," said Lee.

Agnes waved an impatient hand—soccer, football, he knew it was all the same to her.

"Matter of fact," said Lee looking at his watch, and pushing his chair away from the table, "I'd better get going if I want to be on time. Thanks for supper. See ya later." The game wasn't for another hour, but Agnes didn't need to know that. Besides, he'd caught a whiff of Agnes's banana brick baking in the oven and his day had been heavy enough without adding a ten-pound slice of that stuff on top.

He went outside and waved the leash at Santiago. "Come on, girl." She came bounding toward Lee and he snapped the chain onto her collar, slipped the leash over the handlebar of his bike, and jumped on. Santiago gave one of her "Yes!" yips and ran alongside the bike. The soccer complex wasn't more than a twenty-minute ride from his house, so he pedaled slowly and tried to let the breeze blow the film of this crappy day from his skin. When he got there, he locked his bike to the chain-link fence and ambled over to the empty stands. He sat at the far end of the lowest bleacher so he could keep Santiago in the grass beside him. There was still loads of time, so, what the heck, he unclipped the leash and let Santiago run free for a while.

It felt kind of good sitting there in the sun, watching his dog chase butterflies and dandelion fluff. Lee made a frame with his thumbs and index fingers, looked through the imaginary movie lens, and panned the length of the field, ending with a close up of Santi—who by now was licking her butt, of all things. Typical.

Lee let his shoulders relax. The sun felt like a soothing hand against his back. "Buck up, kid," he could almost hear it saying. "Things could always be worse." Lee sighed when he noticed the fresh deposit Santiago had thoughtfully left in the middle of the soccer field. Great. Not a pooper-scooper or a plastic bag in sight. Lee fished a potato-chip bag from a nearby trashcan and started toward the healthy-sized heap.

He was just about to bend down and take care of the problem when he heard a voice from behind. "Hey, *Ein*stein!"

Double great. Lee closed his eyes. He recognized the voice: Martin Bassinger—Martin Pain-In-The-Neck Bassinger from his math class.

"What're you doing in my neck of the woods?" asked Martin, tossing a baseball and catching it neatly in his glove.

"You live around here?" said Lee.

"'Cross the street," said Martin. "Just killing time till Charlotte shows up." He gave a sly smile. "Homework, know what I mean?"

Triple great, thought Lee. Charlotte was all he needed now. Was there a full moon, or what?

"I'm just giving my dog a run," said Lee. He had no intention of saying anything about the soccer game. With any luck, Martin would wander back home to wait for Charlotte and he'd be left to watch the game in peace.

Martin stood there, tossing the ball for a second, as if making up his mind whether or not to say something. Lee was relieved when he saw him start a slow saunter away. He waited for it, though—yep, here it comes, thought Lee, as he watched Martin slow down and turn to say something. "Nice performance this afternoon, Einstein. It was worth the look on old Wood-tic's nerdy-turdy face."

Lee had no idea if that was meant as a compliment or a jab, and really, he could have cared less. It took him a while to maneuver the dog poo into the potato-chip bag. There was no way he could turn the greasy little thing inside out, so he had to use a stick to coax the poop into the bag. Argh. He was nearly at the garbage can at the other end of the field when he heard the last voice on earth he wanted to hear.

"Do you share?"

"Huh?" He looked at gorgeous Charlotte Bailey, eyeing his potato-chip bag.

"Come on, just one," she said. "Salt 'n' vinegar's my favorite."

The way she said it almost gave Lee the dizzying feeling that gorgeous Charlotte Bailey was *flirting* with him, but of course, that was about as likely as *Iron Man* magazine phoning him up for a photo shoot. *Yeah, Lee, we'll pay you a thousand bucks for just one picture of you and those amazing pecs ...*

Lee suddenly gave his head a shake and realized what Charlotte was asking for. Oh, no. He quickly hid the poo-filled salt 'n' vinegar bag behind his back, all too aware of what he looked like: a two-year-old, too spoiled to share his potato chips. But what was he supposed to do? He stared at her and swallowed hard. No words came. Big surprise.

Gorgeous Charlotte Bailey looked at Lee as if there was something seriously wrong with him and walked away, shaking her head. Lee's shoulders drooped nearly to his knees. He watched for a while as Charlotte left the park and headed for Martin's house. "Santi?" he said, still looking at Charlotte's beautiful backside. "You wanna know what Charlie Chaplin once said?" He glanced at Santiago's uncomprehending eyes. "Give me a break," he said. "You know ... Chaplin? The little dude with the mustache and bowler hat? Used to twirl a stick? Whatever. The guy said, 'Life is a tragedy when seen in close-up, but a comedy in long-shot.'" Lee squatted, held Santiago's sloppy jowls in his hands, and looked into her eyes. "You think I'll ever look back on this and laugh?"

Santiago gave a woof.

"Nope," said Lee, "neither do I."

Lee thought about the beginning of this day that seemed so full of possibility. "I'm fine," he said to himself, wishing he could believe it. "I'm totally freakin' fine."

It was then he saw the ribbon that had fallen from Charlotte's ponytail and slipped to the grass like a silky secret. He raced over, picked it up, raised his hand in the air. He opened his mouth, but her name got caught in his throat. Lee looked at the purple ribbon in his hand, lifted it to his nose (oh gosh, no, the smell of wildflower shampoo), and stuffed the ribbon in his pocket without saying a word.

Gravitation can not be held responsible
for people falling in love.
– Albert Einstein

You don't get to choose, you just fall.
– Unknown

CHAPTER FIFTEEN

{
**If winning isn't everything,
why do they keep score?**
– Vincent Lombardi
}

Soon, members from both teams started arriving in twos and threes. When Slang showed up on the other side of the field, Lee saw him shade his eyes and search the stands. When he spotted Lee, he whistled with his fingers and waved. That cheered Lee a little. He watched the team go through their drills. It was a thing of beauty, really. Slang controlled that ball as if he were the master and it the loyal servant, ready to do anything he wished. His moves seemed so effortless, but of course they weren't. Lee wasn't stupid enough to believe that skill like that came without years of hard practice. Still, Slang seemed *born* to connect with that ball.

Santiago just about went bonkers when the game finally began. Lee had to hold tight to the leash or she would have been on that field racing after the ball with the best of them. And she wasn't the only one who was swept away. When Slang got a breakaway in the first ten minutes of the game and scored a wicked-beautiful goal, Lee leapt to his feet with the rest of the crowd, and the contagious rush of excitement was enough to make him forget all about Charlotte Bailey and the salt 'n' vinegar poop incident. It even made him dare to think that maybe this day didn't have to be a write-off after all. That, maybe, just maybe, it could end as spectacularly as it had begun.

Lee watched as Slang's teammates mobbed him after the goal and bombarded him with a storm of back-whacks and high-fives. Those who were too far away raised fists of victory in his direction—"Way t'be, Kischuck!" The ball was brought back to the center line and the ref started the new play with his whistle. Bing-bang, back and forth, a tackle here, a tricky deke there, *oooof!*—a body-check, a whistle for rough play. The speed! Lee found his jaw hanging open half the time.

It took the other team twelve minutes and a few dirty plays to finally break through the Eagles defense and score a goal of their own. At the time, Slang was taking his turn on the bench, but Lee could see that he was just about busting out of his skin to get back out onto the field. When he finally did, he was like a dynamo possessed. He quickly got possession of the ball, faked out his opponent with some fancy footwork, and passed to a forward who took a shot on goal. The goalie dove toward the ball, deflecting it with the tips of his fingers. Slang took the rebound on his forehead and sent the ball sailing smoothly over the downed goalie.

Man, oh man! When that happened, the old guy beside Lee jumped up so fast his popcorn went flying through the air like confetti. Then he turned and hugged Lee, just about lifting his feet from the ground. "Oh Lord, look at me," he apologized when he realized he'd just hugged a complete stranger. "Sorry, kid,"—he straightened the cap on Lee's head—"it's just, well, that's my son out there. He's something, isn't he?" The man didn't wait for a reply. His attention was back on the field and his son, and for a while, Lee watched his beaming profile instead of the action.

Slang's dad, eh? Hmm, pretty nice that some people get to grow up with one of those. He noticed another player's father filming the game with a video camera—not an *ima*ginary one, either. Thank goodness we're not *all* nutballs, thought Lee. Maybe it was the sight of those proud fathers, or maybe just the crappy day catching up with him, but it was about then that Lee began to notice something wrong with his mouth. Not his mouth, exactly, but his *smile*. It felt like it was pasted on his face, like he had to concentrate on keeping it there, or it would just slide right off.

Lee squatted down and pressed his forehead to Santiago's. "What's up with me?" he whispered. Then he spoke to her telepathically, like he often did. *We're here at a soccer game, Santi, and we're winning, and Slang is flying, and I'm thinking about my* mouth? Santiago barked and broke away to sniff at another chained dog, who was far more interesting than Lee at that moment. Lee sighed, straightened up, and tried to concentrate on the play.

As the game continued, the Eagles held onto their win, the fans roared, Mr. Kischuck spilled more popcorn, and Lee should have been flying higher than a kite in a windstorm. He tried telling himself he was: I am. I'm fine. I'm higher 'n a kite. To prove it, he attacked Santiago the way he always did when he was in an extra good mood. He scruffed her behind the ears, let her lick his face, and talked to her out loud this time. "This is the *best*, eh, Santi?! Are those guys un*believable*, or what?" But as the words slipped from Lee's mouth, they made him feel like a big fat phony. Not that he didn't mean what he said; he did. He just didn't have the fire inside to back it up. He got the feeling that if someone had opened his mouth wide enough just then and yelled inside: "Hey, anybody home?" the resounding echoes would have gone on forever … *Anybody home … body home … body home … body home?* Hollow as a dead fly on a December windowsill, that's how he felt. That's what this day had reduced him to. For the rest of the game, Lee went through the motions—clapping, smiling, enduring Mr. Kischuk's big bear hugs. But he couldn't fool Santi.

She pushed her snout under Lee's hand and nudged his butt and gave the kind of half-yip, half-whine that usually got her some attention and a few reassuring pats on the belly. But Lee hardly noticed her. The more he watched the unbelievable talent of the players on the field, the more his own little "Technicolor marathon high" of this morning seemed like some kind of idiotic joke.

After the game, Lee summoned every last bit of energy he had to look happy when Slang came striding toward him.

"Hey, that was amazing, Slang! You're the best!"

"Yeah? You think so?" said Slang faking a punch to Lee's shoulder. "Well, let me tell you something, little bro: I think you must be my good luck charm. You'd better be here for the next game, you hear?"

Lee just smiled.

"You okay?" said Slang. "You look kind of ..."

"I'm f ..." Lee stopped. He couldn't say the word "fine" one more time today. "I'm f ... eeling kind of tired," said Lee. "You know, the marathon and everything."

"Know what you mean, man. Do you need a ride?"

"No, thanks, I've got my bike. See ya, Slang."

"Hey," called Slang, "you've got my phone number, right? Next game's a week today!"

Lee just gave a backward wave and headed for his bike.

I'm not always depressed: only when I think and feel.
– Ashleigh Brilliant

When the morning's freshness has been replaced by the
weariness of midday, when the leg muscles give under
the strain, the climb seems endless, and suddenly nothing
will go quite as you wish—it is then you must not hesitate.
– Dag Hammarskjöld

CHAPTER SIXTEEN

Lee didn't think about much of anything on his way home. For the first time today, it felt good to be empty inside. Just like that dead fly carcass. Blow on it, and poof ... gone like dust.

He just wanted to be at home in his room, lying on his bed, mindlessly tossing a ball to the ceiling and catching it over and over and over again. That's why he surprised himself when he spotted Rhonda walking down the street and decided to follow her at a distance. He leaned his bike against a tree, made sure Santiago's leash was tight on the handlebar, and told her to stay. "I'll be back in a minute, girl." Santiago didn't mind. The smell of a dozen dogs that had visited this tree before had her intrigued.

Rhonda was clomping down the sidewalk in her goofy huge running shoes, carrying a backpack in one hand, and her guitar case in the other. She was humming some crazy tune, off *key*, of course. Lee knew she was on her way to guitar lessons. She took guitar at St. Ignatius, the same school he'd taken saxophone lessons (yeah, *saxophone*) two years ago. The school opened its doors once a week in the evenings for private music lessons. He watched her go in, then sat on the front steps to give her time to get to her lesson. *What goes on inside that girl's brain?* he wondered. Lee wished he could sneak a video camera inside her head and take a good look around.

INTERIOR OF A GIRL'S HEAD: TAKE ONE

CAMERA THREE, START WITH A CLOSE-UP OF THE BUBBLEGUM

STUCK IN RON'S HAIR

The worms crawl in, the worms crawl out, through the eyeballs and out the snout ..." Rhonda could never quite remember the correct tune to that song. Bummer, 'cause she liked it. As she got closer to the school, she stopped humming and sighed. She pushed through the front doors and headed straight for the girls washroom. Rhonda laid her guitar case across the sinks and threw her backpack on the floor. Of all the music teachers in the world, why did she have to end up with a goon who insisted that "a young lady should always wear clothing worthy of the instrument she plays?" In other words, put on a dress and comb your hair before you step into my classroom, missy, or you're out the door.

Rhonda rifled through her backpack and pulled out a stupid, idiotic dress and tried putting the stupid, idiotic, stupid, stupid, idiotic ... (at this point, her arms and head were good and stuck inside, since she hadn't bothered to undo the zipper) stupid,

stupid, idiotic, ugly-hideous thing on over her T-shirt and shorts. The struggle left her with a red face and flyaway hair that nearly touched the ceiling. She looked at herself in the mirror. If only she could keep her high-tops on, it might not be so bad. But she'd tried that a dozen times and been sent back for her shoes— "Those runners are a disgrace, and an insult, Ms. Ronaldson. Out you go." Rhonda had begged her mother over and over again to find a new music teacher, but in the end, even she had to admit that she learned more from Miss Edwards than any other teacher she'd ever had. Rhonda yanked her shoes from the backpack and grudgingly put them on. Then she tried to rake a comb through her tangles.

FADE TO: INTERIOR OF A BOY'S HEAD

ROLL CAMERA

Lee picked at the crumbling cement of the St. Ignatius school steps and finally stood up. The whole saxophone-lesson fiasco of two years ago was not one of Lee's favorite memories. So passing through the school doors that evening didn't exactly bring back a case of the warm fuzzies. And whether he wanted to admit it or not, his conscience didn't feel too good, either. He'd never heard Rhonda play before; she refused to entertain anyone but herself. But he had a feeling she'd suck at it—*big* time—and something in him needed to witness someone *else's* life suck for a second or two and then just walk away.

CUT TO RHONDA

Rhonda looked both ways down the hall before stepping out of the washroom. All clear. She shot down the hall like a fugitive on the run. No way was she going to take the chance of being seen looking like a Barbie doll. Miss Edwards sighed as Rhonda entered. "Miss Ronaldson, have you ever heard of that amazing little invention called the 'iron'?"

"As in, ironing-board and all that? Yeah, I heard of it."

"You might consider using one on your dress before you leave the house next time."

In your dreams, thought Rhonda. The day she'd come out of her house and walk all the way to the school in broad daylight in that dress was the day they'd have to drag her yelling and screaming to the loony bin. She put her guitar case on the nearest desk and opened it.

CUT TO LEE

With rounded shoulders and hands stuffed deep in his pockets, Lee dragged his feet all the way to the music room and put his ear to the door. Nope. Piano music. Maybe she was in the next room. He popped his head into the grade three class but only saw a little kid in there with a flute. Lee walked down the hall, looking into open doors and listening at closed ones. He had thought he'd have no problem tracking Rhonda down; he'd always imagined that she played an electric guitar—an irritatingly *loud* electric guitar—but maybe not. Maybe she had one of those cheap old twangy things that most kids start on.

FADE IN TO RHONDA

"Did you bother practicing this week?"

"Of course," fibbed Rhonda.

"Let's hear it, then," said Miss Edwards, skeptically. "Play the song you were having such trouble with last week."

CUT

ZOOM IN ON LEE

*Fin*ally, thought Lee, coming to a stop, the sound of a guitar. But what he heard outside the door of the grade-eight classroom made him break out into a sweat. Someone in there was playing classical guitar like they knew what they were doing. Like some kind of genius. Lee touched his forehead to the door. No way.

No *way*. That can't be Rhonda. Tell me that's not Rhonda. I don't think I could take it if that was R ... He opened the door a crack and peeked inside. His body instantly relaxed. Whew. It was just some pizza-face kid in there—a dude who had obviously been born with a guitar in his hands. I suppose I should be thankful for small mercies, thought Lee—at least I don't have pimples.

Shoot. This is *pathetic*, thought Lee. What would it matter if Rhonda *did* turn out to be the most talented guitar-pickin' tomboy in the Western Hemisphere? Why did he suddenly have this need for her to be as crappy as him? He hung his head and started down the hall to the exit. He didn't even bother to stop at a door that had some gawd-awful, torturous guitar strumming coming from it. It didn't matter if that was Rhonda in there or not. Nothing mattered.

As he walked, Lee suddenly became aware of a dreamy, far-off whisper of music. It was coming from the downstairs library. Without thinking, he followed the mesmerizing sound down the stairs, like a snake drawn to the flute of a snake charmer. He put his ear to the door. Normally he wasn't the kind of guy who went in for classical symphony stuff, but there was something about this sad-sweet music that pulled him in and wouldn't let him go. Almost like it wasn't music at all, but some kind of growing vine slowly curling its sad tendrils around his heart. Violin. That's what it was.

Lee leaned his back against the door and slowly slid down until his bum met the ground. Any other day he would have been embarrassed to admit he'd been knocked out flat by the sentimental strains of a violin. Right now he was incapable of caring. He closed his eyes and bonked the back of his head against the door. Which turned out to be a colossal mistake. Suddenly he heard a click as the door latch gave way and he found himself lying on the floor looking up at the library ceiling. The music stopped cold.

"Jeez, sorry," he said, scrambling to his feet. He was out the door, about to close it with a final "Sorry 'bout tha—" when he stopped in mid-sentence. The girl playing the violin looked familiar, somehow, sort of like a cleaned-up version of Rhonda Ronaldson. Lee stared. His mouth dropped open. Oh, my gosh …

Rhonda's jaw dropped, too. Her arms fell to her sides, violin dangling from one hand and bow from the other. For a second, you could have heard a pin drop. Instead, *clunk*, they heard Rhonda's bow slip from her fingers to the floor. That was just the calm before the storm. In the next second, Rhonda gathered up all her fury and fired words at Lee like fast-flying spitballs from a straw. "*What* are *you* doing here, ya stupid *jerk*?"

Lee opened and closed his mouth like a fish, but nothing came out.

Rhonda rammed her violin into the guitar case and slammed

the clasp shut. Then she held the case in front of her to hide her ugly dress. "This was *none* of your business, *jerk*-head," she said, pushing past him in the doorway. Lee watched her storm off down the hall. Then he looked at Miss Edwards, who by now had joined him at the door. They both watched Rhonda take her shoes off halfway down the hall and hurl them at the wall. Miss Edwards just shook her head and started gathering up the sheets of music. That's when the truth hit him like a punch to the gut— Lee, Einstein McGillicuddy, son of Frankinstein McGillicuddy, would never be an Einstein, or even a Frankinstein—he would never be fabulously good at anything. He could easily have shrugged it off—the belch and the poop incidents with Charlotte, the failed math exam and the total turd he'd made of himself in Woodtick's class, the embarrassing lame-brain optimism he'd felt at the beginning of the day—*my shirt is toothpaste blue!!!*—gad. Embarrassing, sure, but it was the kind of stuff that might fade, given time. But not *this*—you just don't recover from the certain knowledge that you'll never amount to a hill of stinkin' kidney beans in this life. If even someone like *Rhonda*, of all humanoids, was dripping with talent, he knew he was way too far behind to ever catch up. Might as well give up now.

And that's about when Lee felt his pilot light fizzle out— ff*ssst*—dead; not even the hint of a flame left. He headed toward the exit, numb.

When he got outside, his head rolled back on a limp neck and he found himself looking into the stars.

Einstein?

Frankindad?

Is there anybody up there?

Then he felt a surge of anger. Still glued to the stars, he yelled, "*Who's the director of this piece-of-crap movie anyhow, 'cause it sure as frig ain't me!*"

Human beings, vegetables, or cosmic dust, we all dance
to a mysterious tune, intoned in the distance
by an invisible player.
— Albert Einstein

FADE TO BLACK

CUT

CHAPTER SEVENTEEN

{
When angry, count to four.
When very angry, swear.
– Mark Twain
}

"Frick'n Frack'n F*#!!?/*#@*#." If you'd asked Rhonda why she was so hair-ripping furious ('cause, like, let's face it, it's not as if she'd been caught playing the violin *naked*, or anything), she wouldn't have been able to tell you. No, she would have *refused* to tell you, because she refused to even think about it herself. The word "embarrassed" embarrassed Rhonda. The word "emotions" wasn't in her vocabulary. She wasn't interested in having feelings in the first place, and if she did, she *certainly* didn't want to *talk* about them.

"For the *millionth* time, *nothing's* wrong with me," said Rhonda to her mother.

"Oh, yeah?" said Mrs. Ronaldson. "Then why are you murdering that chrysanthemum?"

Rhonda looked down at the mess of purple petals on the kitchen table. She'd absentmindedly taken one of the flowers from her mother's vase, but she didn't realize she'd been sitting there pulling it to pieces the whole time.

"I'm just bored," said Rhonda, hoping that would put an end to the inquisition.

"You've been cranky for days," said Mrs. Ronaldson. "If you're so bored, why don't you go for a bike ride, or see what Daddy's up to."

"*Daddy*?!" spat Rhonda. "He's the last creep in the world I wanna see."

"Rhonda!" said her mother. "How dare you talk about your father that way!"

Rhonda gave her one of her "he*llo*?" looks. "What's my *father* got to do with this?"

"You just said …"

"Oh," said Rhonda, "*that* Daddy. I thought you were talking about Daddy McGill …"

"Aha!!" interrupted Mrs. Ronaldson. "I suspected as much."

Rhonda gave her mother another "have you gone totally batty?" look.

Her mother continued. "That Beanpole boy has something to do with your foul mood these days, am I right?"

Rhonda opened the fridge and faked looking for something inside, just to hide her face (which by now was as red as the hot-sauce bottle in the fridge door).

"Rhonda," said her mother, her voice softening, "do you have a crush on that boy?"

Crush. *Crush!* Rhonda *hated* that word. It embarrassed her more than "embarrassed." She slammed the fridge door, walked past her mother without dignifying her question with an answer, and walked straight out the front door. Then she saw Lee coming down Agnes's front steps and she did an about-face and came straight back in. She looked at her mother, who was looking back with an amused smile. That did it! She stormed to the back door, slamming it big-time on her way out, and took the long way to school, mumbling under her breath the entire way:

"… a *crush*? On that *'Beanpole boy'*? Give your head a shake, Mother. Are you on *crack*, or what?"

All mothers are slightly insane.
– J.D. Salinger

CHAPTER EIGHTEEN

Hey, Pardner! You've reached the McGillicuddy residence. Neither Gert nor Lee can come to the phone just now. Be a pal and leave a message after the beep.

Beep!

Hey, Lee, Slang here. Missed you at the game last night, Buddy. Everything okay? Gimme a call.

Beep!

Hi, this is a message for Lee. Yeah, Lee, it's Frank here, from Frank's Meats and Deli. You haven't been in for your dog bones lately. Hope Santiago's okay. Just chopped up some fine prime rib and I'll save the bones as usual. Give me a call if you're having canine trouble.

Beep!

Frank again. Meant to say howdy to Gert. Howdy, Gert! Keep a seat warm for me at the club! It's been a while.

Beep!

Hi, Lee. It's Slang again. How come you're not answering

your messages these days, man? Not sick or anything, I hope. Championships coming up. Can't be without my good luck charm. Gimme a call.

June 25
Dear Mrs. McGillicuddy:

I thought I'd drop you a note to let you know that I've been a little concerned about Lee lately. As you know, I've been Lee's homeroom teacher for nearly two years now, and I'll confess to you, Mrs. McGillicuddy, that although we teachers are not supposed to have favorites, I've always had a special soft spot for Lee. Although he's not one of my most academically talented students, he has a sparkle and a generous spirit that shines brighter than most. That's why it troubles me to have noticed a change come over him recently. The spark seems to have left his eyes, and although he's completing homework and handing in assignments, he does so with a certain lifelessness that has me worried. I don't mean to alarm you prematurely, Mrs McGillicuddy. As we both know, it is perfectly natural for children to move through brief rough patches as they grow. But it is the intensity of his "lethargy" this past week that prompts me to contact you. I don't mean to pry, Mrs. McGillicuddy, but is he having any personal difficulties lately that it might be helpful for me to know about? I'd love to be of some help to Lee, but he doesn't seem open to talking right now. I'm leaving you with my home phone number, and that of the school's guidance counselor, and although the final week of school is always a busy one, we wouldn't dream of not making time for you. Lee is a wonderful boy, Mrs. McGillicuddy, and I long to see his big goofy smile light up our schoolroom again.

Sincerely,
Margaret Burns

June 26

Dear Stupid Diary,

I decided to start talking to Lee again, not that he deserves it, the stinkin' spy. But he's totally weirding me out. He's too nice. Well, maybe not nice exactly, but completely unbuggable, if you know what I mean. He didn't even get mad yesterday when I expertly zinged his dumb baseball cap right off his head with my slingshot (no one is better with a slingshot than the Amazing Ron Ronaldson, in case you didn't know, Stupid diary.) He just picked up his hat and put it back on his head like it never happened. He didn't even try to catch me and give me a knuckle noogie to the head.

Actually, I don't think the guy is Lee at all. I think he's some kind of zombie just pretending to be Lee. Or maybe some green aliens picked him up one night and sucked all the personality out of his body before kicking him off the spaceship. Not that he was ever Mr. Personality to begin with, but you know what I mean, right, Stupid?

Yours truly,
Ron, aka The Amazing One

Dear Almighty Director (whoever you are and wherever you are),
This is to inform you that I, Lee McGillicuddy, officially resign from my starring role in this inferior movie called "My Life." I don't like the way the plot is unfolding. If I am the "hero" of this picture, then where are my scenes of heroism?

Nope, the whole production has ceased to be any fun—and, like, I'm not even getting paid (unless you count my allowance, which is beans-all). If you refuse to release me from my role, I'll have no choice but to go on strike till the script shows signs of improvement.

Yours sinc ...

"Oh, my God," said, Lee, letting the pencil drop from his fingers. "I really *am* mental."

CHAPTER NINETEEN

LEE'S CRAPPY LIFE: TAKE 379

MONTAGE SEQUENCE COMING UP

CAMERA ONE, START WITH A TIGHT SHOT OF THE DOG'S DRIPPING DROOL.

QUIET ON THE SET ANNNND, ACTION!

Woof! Rrrrrrrrr, woofwoofwoof!! Howwooooooo!

For a dog, Santiago was pretty smart. But she had the worst short-term memory in the history of dogdom. Long-term memory? No prob. She still remembered, as a puppy, looking out through the bars of her cage at the Humane Society, while a guy in a cowboy hat tried to convince his wife to have a heart: "Come on, Gertie, honey-pie, our son deserves a pet. *Every* boy should have a dog. And just look at that little feller ..."

Santiago remembered that day six long years ago like it was yesterday, but if you'd asked her what she'd eaten for breakfast this morning, she wouldn't be able to tell you, and not just because she couldn't talk English. She simply would not remember. Of course, that bad memory had its advantages at times. She'd bury a bone in the morning, for example, then rediscover it in the afternoon, with a flurry of excited tail-wagging, like it was a brand new find.

But there were also times when her poor memory put her at a distinct disadvantage. Like every day in the past two weeks when she'd rushed to meet Lee coming home from school and had to rediscover anew that Lee wasn't much interested in her these days—that he hardly noticed she was there. Each time it felt like a rude shock. It upset her stomach and made her want to hide under the huge rhubarb leaves in the back yard and go to sleep. Not to mention the fact that Lee hadn't brought her a juicy bone for ages. Howwwoooooow!

CUT TO AGNES'S KITCHEN

The Bluebird of Happiness long absent from his life,
Ned is visited by the Chicken of Depression.
– Gary Larson (cartoonist and creator of The Far Side*)*

"Do you think he might be depressed?"

"Depressed? At his age?" said Gertrude, refilling her coffee cup from the pot on Agnes's table.

"It's possible," said Agnes, pulling a tissue from the sleeve of her housedress and giving her nose a quick honk. "Even kids can sometimes drop into a hole that's hard to climb out of."

"No. It's more likely some kind of growth spurt that's just taken everything out of him. He's grown another inch and a half in the last month, have you noticed? That's gotta be hard on a body."

"Speaking of which," said Agnes, "don't you think it's time to get the boy some new jeans? The ones he's walking around in are short enough to get him through the next Red River flood without getting wet. In fact, maybe he's just embarrassed about looking like a goof."

Gertrude didn't even hear Agnes's last comment. She was too busy thinking. "I had a talk with his teacher yesterday. She agreed that a growth spurt might have something to do with it. Or hormones, maybe. Or both."

Agnes ignored Gertrude right back and continued on with her own train of thought. "I've heard about a herbal remedy that's good for lifting the spirits. St. John's Wort, I think they call it. Maybe ..."

Gertrude looked up over her coffee cup. "Forget it, Ag. Witch's warts and eyes of newts are not what's needed here. Don't go wasting your money on crazy potions. I mean it, Ag."

CUT TO INTERIOR OF "FRANK'S MEAT AND DELI"

Frank took a bag full of week-old beef bones from the fridge and dropped them into the garbage can with a sigh. Then he took a fresh plastic bag from under the counter, filled it with today's bones, and set them on a shelf in the fridge. Before turning off the lights to the store, he stopped to look at a crooked Polaroid snapshot, stuck to the cash register, of a skinny kid and his maniac dog. Frank smiled and straightened the picture before leaving the store and locking the door behind him.

CUT TO AGNES

Agnes set the bottle of St. John's Wort on the counter beside the sink. Then she bent her stiff back to peek inside the oven at the loaf of banana bread she was baking especially for Lee. She knew it was his favorite.

CUT TO SLANG

Slang put his date book in his backpack and got ready to leave his house. Then he took the organizer back out and flipped to tomorrow's date. There he wrote a reminder to himself: *Drop by Beanpole's place sometime soon.* He was about to put the book back in his backpack when he took it out one more time: *Remember to bring a team T-shirt for the kid. Size?* Slang thought for a second, then smiled and continued writing: *"S" for skinny.*

CUT TO GERTRUDE

Gertrude folded the two new pairs of extra-long blue jeans she'd bought that day and laid them at the end of Lee's bed. Then she looked at her watch, hoping he'd get home from delivering flyers soon. She flipped through the TV guide in search of a funny movie the two of them might watch together. Gertrude put a pack of popcorn in the microwave. She parted the living room curtains and looked down the street.

CUT TO LEE'S TEACHER

Mrs. Burns put down her red marking pen, stretched, and went to the kitchen to pour another cup of tea. She carried it back to the dining room table, sat down, and flipped through the messy pile of creative writing essays she'd just finished marking in time for report cards. She took a sip of tea, scratched her cat, Tigger, behind the ear, and put the cup down. Mrs. Burns sorted through the papers until she came to Lee's and, with her red pen, changed the "C" to a "B." She took another sip of tea, planted a kiss on Tigger's nose, and added a plus sign beside the B. "Our secret, Tigger," she whispered.

Rhonda put her violin to her chin and raised the bow. She started playing, but tonight the music made her feel sad. She put the violin down on her bed and peeked through a broken slat in the horizontal blinds at her window. She could see the lights on at Lee's house. She could see Gertrude looking out the front window. She could see Santiago sitting near the front gate. But she couldn't see Lee. Rhonda lay on her bed beside her violin and looked at the cracks in the ceiling.

CUT TO MUTT

Santiago's tail started twitching when she sensed Lee at the end of the block, too far away to be seen. When she felt the mild vibrations of Lee's flyer wagon bumping along the sidewalk, her tail began to thump. When she actually heard his footsteps, her tail wagged so violently she nearly knocked herself over. Of course she'd forgotten. Forgotten that Lee didn't have time for her these days; forgotten that from his point of view, the sun no longer shone from her canine butt—that lately she was just an unremarkable mutt to her boy. Lee came through the gate and gently brushed Santiago away when she jumped up to greet him. "Not now, girl." Santiago waited until he'd gone inside the house, then shimmied under the rhubarb leaves until only her tail showed, and waited for sleep.

SEQUENCE ENDING AS IT BEGAN, WITH A CLOSE-UP OF THE MUTT

CAMERA OUT, AAAAAND ... CUT!

LET'S CALL IT A DAY, FOLKS

CHAPTER TWENTY

{
**There are only two ways to live your life.
One is as though nothing is a miracle. The other
is as though everything is a miracle.**

– Albert Einstein
}

Lee looked out his bedroom window but didn't really "see" anything. Not the sunshine creeping up on his mother's marigolds, turning them into orange balls of fire, not the three blue eggs in the nest under his window that had overnight morphed into three gaping beaks screaming for breakfast, not even Santiago's thumping tail in the rhubarb patch (the opening of Lee's eyes every morning automatically set Santiago's tail a-thumpin'—she sensed his waking even when she wasn't in the same room). Life might as well have been a silent black-and-white movie for all Lee noticed or cared. Black and white. Black *or* white. Either you care or you don't. Simple as that.

And it wasn't so bad, really, this not caring. More like a relief. Lee just wished everyone would stop being so overly worried about him. He didn't like the weight of their concern. It irritated him—the worried look in Agnes's eyes, the way Mrs. Burns had gone easy on him on his final mark (that piece-of-crap essay he'd handed in wasn't fit to line the bottom of a canary cage, let alone earn a B-plus), the very fact that his mother was right now downstairs frying bacon for him—a treat she generally reserved for special occasions. Her little attempts to lift Lee's spirits made him uncomfortable. Not to mention the fact that bacon was wasted on him these days. He didn't have much of an appetite and everything tasted the same, anyway. If Gertrude had served him a bowl of Santiago's Chuck Wagon Vittles, he probably wouldn't have noticed.

Oh, God, Lee closed his eyes, *Santiago.* The thought of her sad eyes these days was enough to make him feel like the biggest crud on earth. Having the power to make or break a dog's day was not a responsibility he wanted right now. And it's not that he didn't love Santiago. Love had nothing to do with this. He just didn't have the energy to fake cheerfulness. Not with her; not with *any*one. Feeling down in the dumps is hard enough, thought Lee, but trying to convince people (or dogs) otherwise takes more energy than running a marathon. *Backwards!*

Lee heard the MSN "ding-dong" informing him that he had a new e-mail. Terrific. He plunked himself down in front of the monitor, although he didn't know why he bothered. These days the only stuff he ever seemed to receive was junk mail (and the odd idiotic note from Rhonda—*Dear Daddy, sorry to hear you've been diagnosed with Zactly Disease—your face looks zactly like your butt! Heh, heh! Your Pal, Ron*).

Lee checked the sender of his latest e-mail—"Angel Wings." *Again!* I can't *believe* this, thought Lee. How many times had he "unsubscribed" himself from this stupid mailing list. Their sappy inspirational messages made him want to hurl. Lee read the message:

AWESOME PRAYER

May today there be peace within you.
May you trust that you are exactly where you are meant to be.

Remember that friends are quiet angels who lift us to our feet
when our wings have trouble remembering how to fly.
Just send this to four people and see what happens on the
fourth day. Do not break this, please. There is no cost,
but lots of rewards.

Lee banged the delete key. If he was exactly where he was "*meant to be*," then life was a bigger joke than he thought.

As he got up to leave, Lee noticed the tip of a familiar scribbler poking out from under his bed—*The McGillicuddy Book of Personal Records*. He flopped heavily onto the mattress and flipped through the pages. Man, oh *man*. Was it possible that he'd aged a hundred years in one week? Suddenly his handwriting looked like it had been scribbled by a six-year-old. He shook his head as he flipped through the pages of idiotic facts, figures, and records. It all seemed so weird and childish now. What thrill had he ever gotten out of being able to say that he'd bounced a stupid basketball for twelve straight hours without stopping? What did it say about him? Only this: that his longing to be good at something, *anything*, had turned him into a fruit-loop crazy enough to believe that any hard accomplishment had the power to transform him. Into *what*? No more than a basketball-dribbling nitwit, thought Lee. Embarrassing. Hu*mil*iating, even.

So that was one good thing about not caring, Lee decided. At least you didn't run the risk of turning yourself into an obsessed nincompoop (accent on the poop). Lee dumped the scribbler into the wastebasket on the way out of his room. The smell of frying bacon in the hallway—along with Gertrude's hope that it would bring a smile to his face—made his shoulders slump. Shoot. He didn't take any joy in disappointing the people around him. Maybe if he just made an effort …

"Yum, bacon!" The sound of his own phony voice made him feel nauseated. No, he just couldn't do it. "Thanks, anyway, Mom, but I'm just not hungry. Give it to Santiago."

There followed a short silence. Then …

"*You* give it to Santiago," snapped his mother, surprising Lee with her impatience. "That poor dog has been half-starved for your affection for weeks. If you can't give her that, then at least give her *this*!" She shoved two pieces of bacon into Lee's hand. It was still hot. Lee felt the heat burning in his cheeks instead of his hand.

As he watched Santiago chaw down the bacon in the front yard, tail wagging a mile a minute, slobber flying, Lee realized that there were some things that he still cared about. Or, at least, *wanted* to care about. What he felt on the inside was his own business. No one could touch that. But the outside was a different story. Okay, so he'd do the hard thing. For the sake of the people around him, he'd break a world record in faking it. Lee Sonny Daddy Beanpole Einstein McGillicuddy breaks an all-time world record for faking a good mood 24/7. God help me.

> *Light up your face with gladness*
> *Hide every trace of sadness*
> *Although a tear may be ever so near*
> *– Charlie Chaplin*

CHAPTER TWENTY-ONE

Rhonda sat on her front steps in the choking sun, chucking tiny pebbles, one at a time, at the petunias lining the front walk. She was aiming at the throats of the dopey flowers—*if I get one in, I'll go say hey to Lee. If I don't, I'll go in and eat some raw cookie dough.* By the time she'd come to the last pebble in her hand, she realized she didn't want to sink the stupid thing—cookie dough was sounding pretty good about now—so, of course, she sunk it.

Rhonda put her chin on her knees and stared down at the caterpillar droppings peppering the concrete steps around her feet. If she kept perfectly still, she could hear the little turds dropping through the leaves. Rhonda brushed off the top of her head, stood up, sighed, and walked toward Lee's house. She could see him digging up dandelion roots with a dull butter knife in his front yard.

Rhonda had learned not to expect much from Lee these days, so she was surprised when he said, "Hey," back and actually smiled. It was a weird smile, mind you—the kind you might give an annoying old relative who expects you to be sweet, and doesn't know a darned thing about you; easier to just give 'em what they want sometimes. But weird or not, at least it was a smile. Rhonda gave a cautious one in return. For all she knew, this was some kind of trick of his to draw her in, just to knock her down.

"Doin' anything?" she asked.

Lee looked at the butter knife in his hand and the pile of dandelion roots by his knees and gave her a "duh?" look.

"Yeah, well," she said, "can't ya think of anything better to do than that?"

"Like what?"

Rhonda thought about saying something totally insulting just then, so he'd be forced to chase her, just like in the old days. Instead, she played it cool.

"I dunno, bike ride or something?" She waited for him to laugh in her face.

"Sure."

Sure. That's what he said, just like that. Not "Take a hike, pipsqueak," or "In your dreams, dumbo." Just, "Sure." This was too easy. It made Rhonda nervous. And anyway, now that he'd said yes, she realized she didn't even *want* to go for a bike ride with Lee McGillicuddy. She'd only wanted to pester him a bit.

But Lee was already up and brushing the mud from his knees as he headed toward his bike. He stopped and looked over his shoulder at Santiago. Might as well kill two birds with one fake stone, thought Lee. He whistled for Santi like he used to, and she came bounding toward him.

Lee slipped Santiago's leash over his handlebar and walked his ten-speed over to Rhonda's side of the street. He waited at the end of her front walk. Rhonda wondered what she could do to get out of this, but couldn't think of a thing. She pulled her own bike from the weeds by the fence and got on.

"Where to?" she asked.

"Name it," said Lee.

Oh, man, what was *up* with him? When was the last time he'd ever let *her* decide anything? Now she was sure he was cooking up something evil. Well, good, thought Rhonda. I like it better that way. She rode ahead, with no particular destination and tried to prepare herself for the prank he was surely about to pull.

When she'd ridden for almost twenty minutes, and found herself nearly at Roblin Boulevard, she looked behind, half expecting to find him gone. He was there, though, and as soon as he noticed her looking, he gave her that idiotic smile again. The next time she looked around, the smile was still there, as if pasted permanently on his face. It was fake. You didn't need to be Einstein to figure that out. And it infuriated her. To have Daddy McGillicuddy, of all people, following her blindly like some mindless, blockhead puppet disgusted her. And disgust always made Rhonda merciless.

Fine, *vacuum head*, you're going to follow me like some idiotic *puppy*, I'll lead you so far your legs'll fall off from pure exhaustion. And she picked up the pace and rode like the wind. She made it all the way to the tracks at Wilkes Avenue before realizing that if she were going to force Lee's legs to fall off, her own would be hitting the dust in the process. As she slowed her pace, she could almost hear the muscles in her calves gasping for breath and cursing her name. This was ridiculous.

Rhonda squeezed her hand brakes for all they were worth and sent gravel spraying everywhere.

Lee burned to a stop just inches from her back fender. Rhonda swung a leg over the crossbar of her boy's bike, dumped it in the gravel on its side, and marched over to Lee. She was about to let him have it, give him a piece of her mind, tell him to stop acting like a loser and more like the self-respecting jerk she used to know. She intended to knock the wind out of him with her words, give him something to think about, maybe even use a few choice swear words. She opened her mouth to do just that, but what she saw on Lee's face stopped her cold. Rhonda had seen the same thing in her own mirror once or twice in her life. She knew what it was, that clean little trail cutting its way through the Wilkes Avenue dust on Lee's cheek. She knew the telltale signs of a tear. Oh, no. No no no no no no no. No way. This isn't what she'd bargained for. She'd known Lee for a long time. She guessed that meant she must care about him. But dealing with his *stuff—anybody's* personal stuff—was something she wasn't made for. There were shoulders in this world meant for crying on, and hers definitely wasn't one of them. Rhonda had always imagined that if her shoulder got wet, she'd melt away like the Wicked Witch of Oz. *"Help me. I'm shrinking, I'm shrinking!"*

Rhonda closed her mouth, turned around, pulled her bike from the side of the road, and got on.

"What are you doing?" called Lee, out of breath.

"Going home. I forgot, I have some things to do." She started to ride, then looked back. Rhonda could see Lee standing on the side of the road, taking a puff from his asthma inhaler with one hand and patting Santiago's head with the other. Suddenly she felt painfully sorry for him. Great. Almighty, frickin', frackin' great. Rhonda turned her bike around and slowly pedaled back to Lee.

The only way to have a friend is to be one.
– Ralph Waldo Emerson

CHAPTER TWENTY-TWO

{ **Don't wish me happiness. I don't expect to be happy all the time ... It's gotten beyond that somehow. Wish me courage and strength and a sense of humor. I will need them all.** }

— Anne Morrow Lindbergh

Lee was less than thrilled to see Rhonda heading back. He'd been doing the good-humor thing for less than an hour now, and already the weight of it felt heavier than the asthma currently pressing down on his chest like an elephant. Truth be told, he wished Rhonda would just go home, but when his asthma got this bad, it wasn't a smart idea to be left alone in the middle of nowhere. A few trips to the emergency ward in the middle of the night had taught him that.

"You okay?" asked Rhonda.

"Yeah," said Lee, feeling the Ventalin already easing some of the pressure in his chest. "I just need to rest a bit."

Lee and Rhonda looked across the tracks at miles of open field once used for farming. The only thing to break the monotony of the blowing prairie grass was an old weathered barn in the distance, with a swayback roof that surely sagged even lower than Lee's spirits. Looked like one good gust of wind could have reduced its sorry old gray bones to a heap of rubble. They headed toward it through the long grass.

"I should have brought water," said Lee, after they'd been walking for what seemed like forever. Santiago's tongue was nearly touching the ground (which didn't seem to matter to her; she looked happier—more quenched—than she had in days).

"Looks like there's an old well over there," said Rhonda. "Let's see if there's any water in it."

Lee knew that there was about as much chance of water in that well as good cheer in the cockles of his heart right now. But he followed Rhonda anyway, stepping over a rusted barbed-wire fence and picking his way through the long, stiff grass. He knew Santiago would come out of this day five pounds heavier in burrs alone, and he also knew who'd have to spend hours cutting them out of her fur. As much as it wasn't in him to devote hours to someone *else's* well-being when his own was in such a cruddy state, he knew it would probably be a good thing. Santi deserved better than what he hadn't been giving her lately.

"Cool," said Rhonda when she reached the well. Bricks were missing from the rim in places, the mortar crumbling, and there were cobwebs across the mouth of the hanging bucket, but it was the kind of thing you might take a picture of, thought Lee, if you were that way inclined. Lee liked old things. He had an instinct to leave them undisturbed—let Time be the artist and work its changes. But Rhonda was different. She liked to fiddle. She liked to leave her mark on the world as sure as Santiago was leaving hers near the corner of the old barn right now.

"Look at this," she said, cranking the handle of the shaft and watching the bucket rise. She dropped a stone into the well—no wet plunk, just a dismal echoing clink as the rock hit the bottom, and from the time it took to land, Lee judged that this well was good and deep.

"You're outta luck, girl," called Rhonda to Santiago, who by now was checking out gopher holes. Lee sat on the edge of the well and rested his head against the post. He watched Rhonda nosing around the well. He was glad she'd found something to take up her attention. Lee knew how awkward his moodiness made her feel.

"I'm going to check out that barn," she said. "Anyone coming?" Santiago was the only one to take her up on the offer. Lee watched them bound through the knee-high grass toward the barn and disappear around the corner. He could hear Rhonda chattering away to Santiago. He hoped she wouldn't go and do something stupid—put her foot through a fool floorboard in the loft or something. He didn't have the energy to fish her out of a mess today. Lee lay in the grass near the well and closed his eyes.

The sun felt surprisingly good. Lee tried looking at the inside of his eyelids—brilliant blood red when he squeezed his eyes tight, mellowing to a puke-orange with firefly flashes of blue and yellow when he relaxed them. And if he looked far enough down to where his lids just barely met, he could see a strip of blue-white light that glowed like the end of the Luke Skywalker laser he used to shine from his bed at night. Lee hadn't done this kind of eyelid watching for years, and strangely, the white light filtering into his brain felt like something he'd needed for longer than he knew. By the time he half-realized that he was slipping into a dream, the light had filled his entire head, and was working its strange magic on his sleepy brain ...

Lee drifts and drifts until he isn't sure if the white light in his head is a state of mind, or a taste, or smell, whether it is his mother's lips upon his forehead, or a soccer ball sailing slow-motion into a net, a foot crossing a finish line, or the lingering note of a violin. Or even the difference between the quiver of a violin's string and the humming of his own vocal chords. All Lee knows is that he is drifting, drifting, upward, like a kite. He can feel the reassuring tug of a string attached to his shirt, though, as if someone—feet planted firmly on the earth—has hold of the other end. And when he feels the string slowly reeling him back to earth, he wonders if he isn't a kite at all, but a fish at the end of a line in an upside-down sea of clouds.

When he's within a meter of the ground, he regains gravity and falls with a soft thud onto the grass. An old man—weather-beaten, sunburned, and smelling not unpleasantly of raw tuna, seawater, and sweat—extends a bandaged hand to Lee. He helps him to his feet, dusts off Lee's shirt and pants, and begins unfastening the string tied to a button on Lee's shirt—the same string he just fished the boy back to earth with. "A wonderful invention, the button, no?" says the old fisherman with a sly twinkle and a wink. He gives Lee the once-over from head to toe, sweeps a stray strand of hair from Lee's eyes, the same way a proud father might before raising the camera to snap a picture of his kid with a trophy.

"I think you're ready," says the old man, pushing Lee gently forward. Lee wonders where exactly he's supposed to go, when suddenly, right before his eyes, the ground trembles and belches out a mighty stone staircase that stretches straight up into a mess of lethargic July clouds.

Lee takes a deep breath and begins climbing … and trudging … and climbing until, hours later (or has it only been nanoseconds?), he hears the distant muffled sounds of a celebration—a dinner party, maybe—laughter, the clinking of glasses, lively music. The sound grows clearer, more crystal, with every stair he takes. Suddenly he's in reach of a huge oak door—"should I open it?"—but the door flies open on its own, drenching Lee in a wave of bright lights and sounds and tantalizing smells. His taste buds sit up and beg for the first time in weeks. "Lee!" A laughing bride (oh my gosh, could that be gorgeous Charlotte Bailey?!) in a white flowing gown runs up and takes Lee's hand, inviting him in as if he is a long-awaited guest of honor. Lee blushes, looks around at the hundreds of wedding guests, wishes he could escape their attention, wonders if he's remembered to put his clothes on today, too terrified to look down and find out. It would be just his luck to find himself in the middle of one of those idiotic dreams where he shows up for school buck-naked.

In the middle of the crowded room, Lee notices someone beckoning. "Me?" he says, looking over his shoulder. Lee is hesitant but his feet obey. He's headed toward a hubbub on the dance floor—some sort of wedding ritual—a hundred guests or more holding hands in a huge circle, dancing round and round, laughing, singing, kicking up their heels. Two of them part hands to allow Lee to join in. Lee balks—even in his dreams he'd rather receive a severe butt-kicking than have to get up on the dance floor.

Just as he's about to sneak away, he once again notices the beckoning stranger again, standing at the center of the whirling circle. The flashing disco ball on the ceiling catches his face, lighting up a full head of crazy-wild white hair. Holy crud, it's ... oh, my gosh, no way ... is it? ... yes ... It's Albert Einstein ... And he's smiling and nodding at Lee to join him. For anyone else, not a hot chance, but for Einstein, he'll dance. You bet.

Lee tries joining the circle, but the dancers' hands remain locked. "Come join us," calls Einstein.

"Us?" Lee now sees that Einstein is holding the hand of none other than Slang Kischuck, dressed in full soccer attire, and Kischuck is holding the hand of Rhonda's dad, who happens to be dressed in nothing but boxing gloves and a "Kiss the Cook" apron tied around his bare gut. The three gold medals dangling from his neck sparkle and wink in the light of the turning disco ball.

Lee tries madly to get through—lemme in!—but no go. He tries ducking under the dancers' arms, but as he does, he catches a glimpse of who's beside Einstein playing the music. It's Rhonda Ronaldson, with her violin tucked neatly under her chin and— get this—Santiago at her feet, looking up at her with the most sickening case of loyal canine devotion he's ever seen.

"Santi!" he calls, "how dare you? Santiago, get your sorry tail-wagging butt over here! Right now!! I MEAN IT!!!"

"What's your problem?" said Rhonda. "She's just chasing a gopher, cryin' out loud."

Lee looked up at Rhonda. What the …?

"Were you *sleeping*?" she said. The level of disgust in her voice told Lee Rhonda was feeling better. The barn exploration must have revved her up a notch or two. Lee rubbed his eyes.

"Yeah, I guess I must have dozed off for a second," said Lee, trying to hold onto his dream that insisted on escaping faster than a slippery frog in a pair of greased hands.

How can you determine whether at this moment we are sleeping, and all our thoughts are a dream; or whether we are awake, and talking to one another …

– Plato

CHAPTER TWENTY-THREE

{
**Depend on the rabbit's foot if you will,
but remember it didn't work
for the rabbit.**

– R.E. Shay
}

{
**The only sure thing about luck
is that it will change.**

– Bret Harte
}

"Look what I found," said Rhonda, holding up an old rusty horseshoe. "It's gonna bring me a turd-load of luck, I can feel it in my teeth." She sat down on the side of the well. "Whoa, looky here," she said.

Rhonda was staring up at a section of rope just below the pulley that was in rough shape. The strands had rotted away and come unraveled so that the bucket was holding on by only a thin thread. It looked as if at any moment they might hear a cartoon-like "ping!" as the rope gave up the ghost, sending the bucket hurtling down the well. Rhonda gave the rope a tug.

"Leave it alone, why don't ya?" said Lee.

"Butt out," said Rhonda, chucking the horseshoe into the bucket. "I wonder how many rocks it would take to snap that baby. Make a guess, Daddy." She smacked a mosquito on her cheek, leaving behind a trail of blood and tiny black body parts.

"Better yet," said Rhonda, "let's have a contest. We'll take turns dumping rocks into the bucket and see who can sink that sucker first." She searched in the grass for the biggest rocks she could find, and piled them in a heap. "Come on."

"Let's just go home now," said Lee. "My asthma is much better now. I think I could ..."

"Don't be a doink," said Rhonda. "Come on. The one who wins has to buy the ice cream on the way home."

Lee didn't have the energy to argue. From the look of the rope, it wouldn't take long to snap, anyway. He picked the biggest rock from the pile and dumped it in the bucket. Rhonda went next. After ten rocks each, they were both amazed at how stubborn that "last thread" was. Lee became a little more interested. He watched Rhonda huck another rock into the bucket. Five more turns each, and Lee stopped to examine the rope. Where was that scrawny piece of string getting the will to hold on under such pressure?

Rhonda went in search of some bigger rocks and came back

hauling a small boulder. This time she climbed up on the edge of the well and dumped the boulder from high up, hoping the jarring effect would be enough to do the trick. *Clunk*. No dice.

"There's more boulders over there," said Rhonda, pointing to a crumbling stone fence. Lee walked toward the wall—anything to keep her quiet—and came back carrying two rocks that made his arms feel like they might drop off. He dumped his own in the bucket. They saw a few hairs of string give way. Lee knew the next rock would do it. He imagined how ticked-off Rhonda was going to be when she found out he didn't have any money for the ice cream.

He handed the rock up to Rhonda. She squeezed her eyes shut, as if silently chanting a little prayer (or curse), before dropping it in. To their mutual amazement, the rope held strong. "Jeez!" Rhonda stomped her foot against the ledge of the well, tantrum-style. What happened next might as well have been an excruciatingly slow-motion film inside Lee's head. He saw Rhonda's foot travel miles through space before making contact with the brick, sending out earthquake tremors— *kabongonnngonngongonngong*—resounding in his brain. He watched the mortar beneath the brick take an eternity to crumble, and he saw Rhonda's foot sl*iiiiiiiiiiiiiiiiiiiiiiiiiii*diing right along with it. Before he could grab at her (his hand felt like a five-thousand-pound weight that would have taken a year and a half to reach her), he watched Rhonda's face disappearing below the rim of the well—her terrified, gaping mouth, her bloody, mashed-mosquito cheek, her shocked eyes. The last he saw of her body was one lone hand grasping at air like a swimmer going under. The sound of the bucket smashing the side of the well as Rhonda brushed past it, and then the sickening thud of her body hitting the ground jerked the film into fast motion.

A thought struck him like lightning—the bucket!!! As Lee looked up at the pulley system, he could actually see the last thread in the rope "pinging" in midair, and he felt himself—like some kind of superhero plucking a speeding bullet out of the air—reach out and catch the end of the streaking rope, stopping it from plummeting into the well on top of Rhonda's head.

Whhhoooooooomph. Lee's gut hit the side of the well as the tonne-weight bucket dragged his arms and head into the well, leaving his stomach balancing on the rim, legs flailing in the air. It was a miracle that his arms hadn't been wrenched out of their sockets. Lee's biceps were like a couple of soft perogies at the best of times, so both he and his muscles were in a state of shock that he was still hanging on to the rope. In his stunned daze, he wondered where the gross animal grunts were coming from before realizing they were escaping his own mouth. He'd had the wind knocked out of him before, but never like this.

By the time he'd stopped gulping and wheezing and moaning

like a cow, the resulting silence sent a cold wave of panic through him. "Rhonda?" he rasped. He could just barely see a dark heap at the bottom of the well. "Rhonda, are you okay?!" No response. "Rhonda! *Say* something. Tell me you're okay!" Lee didn't like hearing the sound of his voice inside this well. The lonely echoes made him feel like the last living person on earth. Lee tried pulling at the rope to lift the bucket out of the well, but it was no use. Even if he'd been strong enough to lift it all the way to the top, he'd never have the strength to navigate it over the edge.

"Rhonda? Come on, tell me you're *okay*, Ron."

Gut-wrenching silence.

Silence is the most powerful scream.

– Anon

CHAPTER TWENTY-FOUR

{
**When you get to the end of your rope,
tie a knot and hold on.**
– Franklin D. Roosevelt
}

Lee squeezed his eyes shut. The blood went rushing to his head. He felt his heart pounding on the door of his chest like a claustrophobic stuck in a dark closet—*Lemme outta here!!* For a second, black blotches started dancing before his eyes. And then, *oh please, no*, his hands started to sweat. And as his palms sweat, his heart beat faster, and as his heart beat faster, his palms sprang fresh leaks.

Get a hold of yourself, Lee. *Get a grip!!*

Lee tried to calm down. He made an effort to breathe slow and steady. Slow and steady. That took care of the black blotches. Then he tried getting his brain to kick in. Something had to give here. His muscles weren't gonna hang on forever. He needed to get some leverage, but with his stomach pressing into the rim of the well, and his feet in midair (like Superman taking a nose dive into a garbage can), the prospects looked grim.

Lee slowly lowered his feet until his toes touched the grass. Then he planted his feet firmly on the ground, with his knees pressed against the wall of the well. Lee took a deep breath and pulled on the rope with all his might.

Didn't budge. Not an inch. Then he saw it: a blessed knot in the rope just a foot or so below his knuckles. If he could just reach that knot … Lee slowly slid one hand down the rope until he had the knot in the palm of his hand. Then he shimmied his other hand down and quickly clasped it over his fist—two hands, as if clenched in prayer, hanging on for dear life.

He waited three seconds, then took another deep breath and as he drew the air into his lungs, a clear picture of Slang suddenly flashed in his head—Slang Kischuk, spent, exhausted, and pain-racked, giving his last ounce of strength to finish the marathon. And that brief flashing picture was as good as Slang handing Lee a Mars Bar. A shot of adrenalin rushed through him. Lee gripped the knot and tried again. This time he used the muscles in his back and thighs as well as his arms.

Quarter-inch by quarter-inch, he pulled the rope and heard the bucket bump-scraping its way up the side of the well, sending little avalanches of mortar and crumbled brick down on Rhonda. With a final heave (like the mother he'd once read about in the newspaper who'd miraculously found the strength to lift a thousand-pound car from her son's trapped body), he pulled on the rope until his arms and head slowly rose out of the well. Standing now, leaning back slightly so that the rope strained against the rim of the well instead of dangling from his spaghetti arms, Lee let out his breath. The bucket still hung down inside the well, but at least he'd bought himself some time.

Santiago chose that exact moment to come bounding toward Lee, all slobbery and happy as a nutcase. She sprang her paws up on Lee's thighs and gave a friendly yelp. Lee snapped. "*Santi*," he yelled, "get *off me*! Jeez, can't you see I'm in *trouble* here?"

Santiago lowered her head and dropped her tail. She took a few steps away from Lee, then stopped and looked back at him over her shoulder. She'd known Lee to ignore her before, and even be impatient with her, but he'd never used that hostile, cutting tone before. If there'd been a rhubarb patch around, Santiago would have slunk under it and stayed there forever. Lee instantly felt bad, but he couldn't think about that now. His mind was racing, trying to figure out what to do next. He lifted one foot from the ground and placed it on the rim of the well. He thought maybe if he pushed hard with his foot, *just like this*, and leaned back with all his weight on the rope, *like that* ... Big mistake. *Bam!* The pressure of Lee's foot broke through the old bricks and sent them flying. As one foot shot through the wall, his other skidded through the grass like a son-of-a-gun. Next thing he knew, he was flat on his back, looking up at the drifting clouds and wondering how the heck he'd managed to keep hold of that rope. Lee wasn't sure if he believed in angels, but as he looked up at the clouds, he felt fairly certain that someone up there was looking out for him.

But he also knew he needed the help of an earthly mortal or two—no doubt about that. He turned his head toward the distant road, where the whizzing cars looked smaller than ants. He called out. "Help! *Help!*" but he knew there wasn't a hot chance he'd be heard, or even seen, for that matter. He looked back into the sky.

Clouds. As far as the eye could see. One that looked like a five-legged dog. Another that bore a striking resemblance to Mr. Wood's fat head. No, this wouldn't do. Lee needed to find a better position. Slowly, painstakingly, making some impossibly tight maneuvers, Lee twisted and shimmied under the weight of the rope until he was sitting upright with his back against the well. The rope cut into his shoulder this way, but it was bearable.

Lee took a minute to catch his breath, then looked around for Santi. "Santiago," he called. "Where are you?"

Santiago didn't budge from her nest in the tall grass. "Santi," called Lee, with a lump in his throat. "Where are you, my girl?"

Santiago lifted her nose. She *wanted* to trust Lee.

"Come on, baby."

Santiago got to her feet and looked across the field at Lee, her tail still drooping as if it had a lead weight tied to the end of it. But that tail started to twitch, then wag, then it pretty much jet-propelled her across the field, all the way to Lee.

Lee wished he could put his arms around his dog. "I'm sorry, Santi," he whispered, offering his face for Santiago to lick. "I'm sorry for yelling at you, and I'm sorry for ignoring you lately …" Santiago happened to be excellent at accepting apologies. Before the sentence was over, she'd already forgiven him. By the time she was finished with Lee's face, she'd nearly licked his freckles off.

"Santi, Rhonda's down that well and she's either knocked out cold, or she's …" Lee couldn't finish the sentence. He called Rhonda's name again, good and loud this time. *"Rhonda! Wake up, Rhonda!!"*

Was it his imagination, or did he hear a sound? "Rhonda?!"

Her words echoed out of the well, weak but distinct. "How many times I gotta tell ya?! That's not my name, Bozo."

"Rhonda??"

"My name's Ron. Get that through your thick skull."

In that second, Lee was glad that good-old-pain-in-the-butt Rhonda Ronaldson was exactly who she was. He could have hugged her, and he just about told her so (boy, wouldn't that have ticked her off!). "Ron, are you okay? Can you stand up? Can you reach the bucket, Ron? Can you carry it down? Are you okay, Ron?"

Santiago got caught up in the excitement and yelped a few greetings of her own down the well. "*Hey, Rhonda,*" she barked, "*Lee's freckles taste extra sweet today. Lick him! Go on, lick him and see for yourself! Howooooooooooo!*"

Then they heard Rhonda cry out in pain. "Ahhhhh, my leg!!" Even Santiago was startled by the panic in her voice. "Ouch. Oh. *Owwwwww!* I can't stand up, Daddy ... I think ... I think it's *broken.*" It sounded like she was trying to strangle a sob creeping up her throat. "Can't you reach down and *help* me?" she called.

"I can't, Ron," he said. "I'm holding onto the rope ... so the bucket won't fall. I can't move an inch."

"Just pull the stupid thing up and get me the heck *out* of here!!" she screeched.

Talk about feeling like a failure. Lee suddenly desperately wished he'd taken up weight lifting instead of wasting all those years breaking stupid, idiotic records. "I can't move, Ron. It's taking all my strength ... just to hang on to this rope." He thought he could hear her crying.

"Are there spiders down here?" she whimpered.

Get *outta* here! Lee wouldn't have guessed in a million years that Rhonda Tough-As-Toenails Ronaldson would be afraid of a spider!

"No," he answered.

"How do you know?" Her voice was trembling now.

"Because," he fibbed, "spiders stop breathing in elevations lower than ground level." Lee squeezed his eyes shut, hoping she'd buy something that lame. "We learned that in science last year."

Rhonda was quiet for a minute, then: "Daddy?"

"What?"

"My head hurts."

"You've probably got a concussion," called Lee. "You were out cold for a few minutes there." He could hear her sobbing now, and he knew she was going to be furious with herself for blubbering in front of him.

"Don't worry, Ron, we're going to get help. I promise."

Lee called Santiago to his side. "Santi," he said, "do you think you can do something for me, girl?" Lee dipped his head and knocked his baseball cap off with his knee. "*Get* it, girl," he said in his "go fetch!" tone of voice. Santiago understood. She picked up the hat in her mouth and brought it back to Lee. Lee lifted one of his feet and gently pushed Santiago away. "Take it to Mom or Agnes, Santi. *Mom* or *Agnes*. Give them the hat and bring them back here. You can do it, girl. Take it to *Mom* or *Agnes*."

Mom. Agnes. The Ladies of the Kitchen. Their very names brought a swift picture into Santiago's mind of a full dish of water and an overflowing bowl of food. Santi was thirsty. She was hungry. Okay! She'd take the cap to Mom, and check out the bowls while she was at it. Santiago took off across the field.

"Good girl, Santi, good girl!! Bring Mom back!"

Lee tried to relax the rock-tense muscles in his shoulders and wondered what he'd done to deserve this. "Comedy, tragedy, cliff-hanger," he mumbled. "When's this movie gonna make up its mind what it wants to be?"

"What'd you say?" called Rhonda.

"Ever imagine your life's an ongoing movie?" he said.

"Huh?"

"Frig, I dunno ... do you ever think you hear a director's voice shouting inside your head?"

"Do I *look* like a weirdo-loser to you?"

Lee thought about the exclusive "weirdo-loser club" he belonged to and wondered if he minded being its only member. He sighed and watched Santi until she was nothing more than a speck on the horizon. No, he didn't think he minded.

"... to be nobody but yourself,
in a world which is doing its best,
night and day, to make you everybody else ..."
– e . e. cummings

CHAPTER TWENTY-FIVE

{ To err is human, to forgive, canine.

– Anon }

{ You think dogs will not be in heaven?
I tell you, they will be there
long before any of us.

– Robert Louis Stevenson }

READY TO SHOOT THE "BOY / DOG" SEQUENCE

CAMERA THREE, A CLOSE-UP ON LEE'S STRAINING MUSCLES

CAMERA FOUR, LOTS OF LOW-TO-THE-GROUND CAMERA WORK

FOR A DOG'S-EYE VIEW OF THE WORLD

READY? AND ... ROLL

Lee's words echoed in Santiago's head—*bring Mom back, bring Mom back.* She stopped just long enough to smell something interesting near the side of the road—big mistake. Cat pee. Very nasty. Santiago trotted on—*bring Mom back, bring Mom back*—

she caught sight of the offending cat up a tree, but didn't bother to stop and bark; she had more important things to do—*bring Mom back, bring Mom back ...*

AND ... CUT TO BOY

> *A table, a chair, a bowl of fruit, and a violin;*
> *what else does a man need to be happy?*
> – Albert Einstein

An hour had passed now, and Lee's back and arms were starting to cramp. Rhonda had stopped crying, but Lee worried about her silence.

"Talk to me, Ron," he said. "Is the pain really bad?"

"I don't feel like yakkin'," she said. "I'm tired. I just want to go to slee ..." He could hear her voice trailing off into dreamland. *Dreamland?!*

"Rhonda!" he shouted. "Don't go to sleep!"

"Cheez ... don't have a hairy fit," she grumbled. "I'll keep you company when I wake up."

"You don't get it," said Lee. "You've got a con*cussion*! You're not supposed to sleep with a concussion!"

"Just for a few minutes, Lee ..."

"*No*, Rhonda!"

"My name's not *Rhonda*," she hissed. Lee scrunched his eyes and shook his head. What was that he was thinking a while back? Something about liking Rhonda exactly the way she was? Must have been a brain fart.

"Rhonda … I mean, Ron. You can slip into a coma if you fall asleep with a concussion. Haven't you ever watched *Rescue Rangers*?"

"Yeah, yeah, okay," she said irritably. "Keep me awake, then. Tell me about something. *Ouch!*"

"What do you want me to tell you?"

"How the heck am *I* supposed to know? I'm the one with the con*cussion*, 'member?"

Lee sighed. He wracked his brain for something to talk about. He wasn't a great conversationalist at the best of times, but with *Rhonda*, of all people?

"Did you know that Albert Einstein played the violin?" he said, finally.

"Yeah?" Lee thought he detected a spark of interest in Rhonda's voice.

"Yeah. He said that if he wasn't a physicist, he would have liked to be a musician."

"You making that up?"

"Nope." Lee shifted his back to stop the rope from cutting into his shoulder. As he did, the rope scraped the rim of the well and sent a rock down on Rhonda.

"Hey, *watch* it!"

"Sorry," said Lee. Then: "Ron, why didn't you ever tell me you play the violin?"

"Shut up," she said. "Tell me something else."

"What?"

"How the heck am I supposed to know? I'm the one with the concuss—"

"Yeah, yeah," interrupted Lee, and he tried to pick his brain for something else that might interest her, but it was as if they spoke a different language half the time.

"Parlay-vous Frances?" he asked.

"Huh?"

CUT TO MUTT

Did you ever walk into a room and forget why you walked in?
I think that is how dogs spend their lives.

– Sue Murphy

Santiago dropped Lee's baseball cap on the ground in order to snap up a Chicken Gui Ku ball on the ground outside of the Wong Numba Café. Ten minutes later, a kid with nothing better to do than pop wheelies in the parking lot got off his bike, picked up the cap, and popped it on his head. By then Santiago was a block away, trying to remember what it was she was supposed to tell Mom …

AND BACK TO BOY …

> *In three words I can sum up everything*
> *I've learned about life: it goes on.*
> *– Robert Frost*

Three hours now, and Lee was beginning to wonder if this day would ever end. His butt was sound asleep and snoring, even if Rhonda wasn't. And a numb bum was the least of his worries. The rope was still cutting a rut into his aching shoulder and cramping his hand. And even *that* wasn't the worst of it. He was running out of topics to entertain Rhonda. Lee was grateful when she came up with a question of her own.

"Why'd you give Santiago that stupid name, anyway?"

"I told you, my dad named her after the old man in *The Old Man and the Sea*."

"So what was so great about this guy that he had to go naming your girl dog after him?"

Lee thought about it. "Do you know the story?" he asked.

"As *if*. You think I go around reading Hemingway? *Ouch!*

My leg!!" Lee grimaced with Rhonda's pain. He knew she needed distracting.

"It's about an old man," he began.

"Duh, no kidding," said Rhonda.

Lee ignored her. "He's an old fisherman in Cuba who's gone eighty-four days in a row without catching a single fish. And he lives in a shack, and his wife is dead, and he uses newspaper to cover the bedsprings because he doesn't have money for a mattress."

"I don't know if I want to hear this story," said Rhonda.

"And here's the kicker, Ron; he's got just about nothing, but he's happy. And hopeful. Every day he goes out in his boat and thinks, today's the day I'm gonna catch a fish."

"And does he?" asked Rhonda.

"Eighty-fifth day," said Lee, "he goes out in his small boat and sails way out past all the other fishermen. And he catches him a fish."

"The end," interrupted Rhonda.

"Nope. This is no ordinary fish story, Ron. The thing weighs fifteen hundred pounds, and it's longer than his boat. It's the biggest darn thing he's ever laid eyes on."

"And he brings the fish home," said Rhonda, "and he sells it for a million bucks, and buys a king-size bed and lives happily ever after. The end."

"Who's telling this story?" said Lee, starting to get irritated.

"Now, have a little patience Rhonda, and I'll tell you what—"

"My name's not Rhonda."

Lee squeezed his eyes shut again and counted to ten. He wondered if Santiago had made it home yet.

CUT TO DOG

Santiago relied on her nose to play the "hot and cold game" to get her home. She didn't recognize the street she was on—Lee had never brought her this way before—but her nose told her which way to go. "Cold," it whispered whenever she took a wrong turn, and "Hot" when she started trotting in the right direction. Santiago stopped to pee by the base of a tree—so many trees, so little time—and turned down a street that made her nose icy. She turned left at the next intersection and knew she was hot on the trail again.

Even though she couldn't recall exactly why, Santiago felt particularly happy this afternoon as she trotted down the boulevard—except for one thing: There was something niggling at the back of her mind like an annoying flea—a little voice telling her she'd forgotten something. Was she supposed to tell Mom something? But the next tree called out to Santiago to leave her mark behind, and as she whizzed, the annoying flea jumped straight out of her mind.

ROLL 'EM

"You see, Ron," said Lee, "the fish was so huge and powerful that once it got caught on the end of the old man's rope, it started dragging the boat out to sea instead of the old man dragging *it* back to shore. There's just no way he could pull the fish in. But the old guy hung onto that rope with all his might, and refused to let go."

Without letting go, Lee flexed the stiff fingers of his hands, one at a time. "So anyway …" Lee stopped. "You still awake, Ron?"

"Yeah," she said, trying to sound bored, but Lee knew he had her hooked.

"For four whole days," continued Lee, "the old guy had a tug-of-war with that fish. It was like some kind of crazy marathon. He had to eat raw tuna to stay strong, and his hands were a bloody mush from hanging onto the rope for so long, and every muscle in his body ached."

"Didn't he ever hear the saying: 'Enough's enough'?"

Lee ignored her again. "And you wanna know the weirdest part?"—he didn't give her a chance to answer—"The weirdest part is that as much as he wanted to kill that fish, he loved it as well. He loved it like a brother. And he loved the moon and stars like brothers, even though the nights were long and painful."

Rhonda made fake gagging sounds at the bottom of the

well. "'The moon and the stars were his brothers.' Lee, I think you've been reading too many romance novels."

Lee smiled to himself. "Could be, Ron; could well be."

"Lee," he heard her say a moment later, "do you think Santiago is on her way back yet? Do you think she understood?"

CUT TO DOG

Some days you're the dog, some days you're the hydrant.
— Anon

Santiago understood perfectly well that squirrels were way too fast to even think about chasing, but they were such irritating little wackos. Always bragging, always teasing—*Hey, dog-chow breath, better watch out or you'll trip on your tongue!*—that's why Santi just had to stop and give that bushy-tailed pest, chittering away on the fence, a good old-fashioned scare. She was fast enough to at least do that. But before Santi had even finished thinking it, the squirrel had hightailed it to the top of a tall tree and sat laughing down at her.

Yesterday I was a dog. Today I'm a dog. Tomorrow I'll probably still be a dog. Sigh! There's so little hope for advancement.
— Snoopy

That's the secret to life ... replace one worry with another ...
– Charlie Brown

Lee's hands hurt so bad, it almost made him forget that anything else in the world existed. Including Rhonda (whenever she'd rest her trap for more than a minute straight—jeez, was it really me who told her not to go to sleep?).

"How'd you get that stupid name, anyhow?"

Lee bristled. "Shadup! Lee is a perfectly ..."

"Not *that* name," said Rhonda. "I'm talking about the *stupid* one: McGillicuddy. Stupid!"

Lee gave a weary shake of the head. "And I suppose you *chose* Ronaldson as your last name?"

Lee imagined Rhonda giving her nose an upward swipe—buying herself just enough time to figure a composed response. "No, dopey," she spat, "but if I could choose, I sure as HECK wouldn't have chosen old fuddy duddy McGillicuddy."

"I'll have you know," said Lee, "that there's no other name I'd rather have. Did you know that the late, great Connie Mack had the very same last name? Well ... before the name-change, that is."

"NOW, THAT'S EXACTLY WHAT I'M *TALKING* ABOUT!!!"

Rhonda chucked a loose stone at the side of the well. "I'd change my name to Mack too if I had to suffer McGillicuddy! Takes a girl to be able to figure something like that out."

"Sorry, toe-brain," sang Lee, "but Connie is a man's name. Not only was he a super-duper professional baseball player, but he was also a legendary major league manager who—"

Lee scowled at the "PPFFFT!" sound that seemed to echo to him from the well. "Baseball, shmaseba—"

Lee cut in. "AND … he held the unbeaten RECORD for most wins …" Suddenly he saw the hopelessness of communicating anything of importance to Rhonda Ronaldson, and gave up. Unfortunately, Lee was able to imagine all too well her Huge-Hairy-Deal smirk. He imagined her eyeballs stuck to the ceiling of her lids right about now.

"So what happened to the old guy, anyways?" asked Rhonda.

"Connie Mack?" said Lee.

"As *if*!" said Rhonda. "I'm talking about the old dude and the fish. Did he have some kind of miracle happen to him or somethin'? That's gonna bug my butt royally, if he had a miracle. I hate it in books when … are you *listening* to me, Daddy?"

Lee hadn't been listening. He was too busy worrying about the cramp in his right hand. He needed so badly to let go of the rope, even for just a second, but he knew he couldn't.

"Daddy?"

"What? Oh. Yeah. What do you want?"

"I *said*, what happened to the old fart, 'cause, like, if you're going to tell me he—"

"You wouldn't want to know, Ron," said Lee.

"Hey, come on, you can't just—"

"Trust me," he said. "You just wouldn't want to know what happened next."

"Well, I'm not going to *beg* you, if that's what you think." He could tell she was ticked.

Lee let ten minutes go by before asking her if she was still awake. She didn't answer, but soon he could hear her chucking pebbles at the side of the well. He wondered what was going through her mind. It was a while before she spoke.

"It's because I'm not ready, if you *must* know," said Rhonda.

"Huh?" Rhonda was constantly coming up with weird things out of the blue, and expecting him to follow.

"You asked why I keep my violin a secret," she said. "It's because I'm not ready, and tough beans to anyone who doesn't like it. I don't want anyone getting the stupid idea that they know me till I'm ready to be known."

"Okay," said Lee.

But Rhonda had more to say.

"Like, imagine you were trying to write the most fantastic story in the world, and for months you put your whole heart and soul into it. And you wrote and rewrote the darned thing, and even though you were far from being finished, you could tell it was getting better and better. And then, imagine that some pea-brain idiot came along one day and stole one of your old, crappy, rough copies from the trash can and *read* it. Wouldn't you just want to tear their *eye*balls out?"

Lee was getting the distinct feeling that either Rhonda, or girls in general, had a different way of thinking about things.

"The point *is*," said Rhonda, "I'm pretty much a rough copy right now, and I don't want anyone trying to read me. Till I'm *ready*. Do you get my drift?"

Silence. He could hear her sigh.

"Man," said Lee, "all I know is that all my life, all I've ever wanted was to be half as good at anything as you are at the violin. If I had one-*tenth* of your talent, I'd be shouting it from the rooftops."

"You're nuts, Lee."

"I know."

"No, I mean, you *really* think you're not good at anything?"

Silence for a count of ten. Lee finally spoke up. "I've gotta tell you something, Ron. 'Member I was telling you about Connie Mack?"

Rhonda went for the bait. "Who's she?"

Lee groaned.

"I know, I know," shot Rhonda, "the baseball nerd. What about him?"

Lee let out a long sigh. "You know I said he held the record for most games won in a lifetime?"

She didn't answer.

"What I didn't tell you," choked Lee, "is that he also held the record for the most losses."

"Wha ...?"

"He just stayed with baseball way longer than any other manager. He may have had a lotta wins, but he had even more losses." Lee closed his eyes. "Guess I was right after all, Ron. I deserve the stupid name."

"Boo hoo." Lee could hear her trying unsuccessfully to chuck a pebble out of the well. "What you're forgetting to remember is that you've got as much piss 'n' vinegar and bull-headed patience inside you as that old dude and his big dumb fish— heck, as stubborn Connie Mack, for that matter. You don't think that's worth something?" she said.

Lee thought for a while, and then he said: "Do you get good marks in school, Ron?"

"Could if I wanted to," she said.

I'll bet you could, thought Lee. "You're pretty amazing, you know that, Ron?"

"Cryin' out loud," said Rhonda, "I am what I am. Now shut

the heck up, and tell me the rest of that dumb story."

I yam what I yam and that's all what I yam.
– Popeye the Sailorman

BRING IN SLANG FOR A SHORT SCENE

QUIET ON THE SET ... AND ROLL!

Slang Kischuk raised his sunglasses over his eyebrows, reached over the back seat of his car, and raked around in the mess of books and garbage until he found what he was looking for—a brand new Eagles team soccer shirt with a bold *McGillicuddy* written on the back, and a number one on front. He looked it over, smoothed a few wrinkles with his hand, and smiled. He got out of his car and then jumped back in and took something from the glove compartment. He tossed the object up in the air and whistled as he walked up Lee's front walk. Then he took the steps three at a time and rang the doorbell. He heard Gertrude's voice through the screen door. "Door's open, partner, come on in!"

Slang opened the screen door and stepped inside. He saw Gertrude wearing a Harley-Davidson T-shirt with the sleeves cut out, cutoff shorts and cowboy boots, and a tool belt around her waist. She was squatting in front of the television's panel box with a screwdriver in her hand. She looked up. "Oh!" she slipped her screwdriver into the loop on her tool belt like a cowboy returning a gun to its holster. "Name's Slang, isn't it?" she said. "Just trying to repair the idiot box, here, Slang. Should be easy enough. Little bit of common sense is all you mostly need. Come on in! Take a load off! Know anything about these fool machines?"

Slang smiled and sat down on the couch. He gave an admiring whistle. "Beauty of a cowboy hat," he said.

"Thanks for noticing," said Gertrude. "It's the real McCoy. Genuine Stetson. Get you a cold drink?"

"No, thanks, Mrs. McGillicuddy," said Slang. "I just came by to give Lee this." He held up the T-shirt. "Genuine Eagles T-shirt for the kid. The real McCoy. Is he around?"

"Well, isn't that kind of you," said Gertrude. "But no, the kid's not around. I keep telling him to leave a note when he goes out, but he can't seem to get in the habit. Haven't a clue where he is, to tell you the truth."

"Well, maybe you could give this to him when he gets home," said Slang, handing over the T-shirt. "Oh, and this, too." He tossed Gertrude a Mars Bar. "Just something I owe him," he said with a wink. "He'll know what it's about."

"Sure thing," said Gertrude, opening the front door for Slang. "But are you sure you can trust me with this?" she said, waving the chocolate bar in the air.

Slang laughed. "Do your best," he said.

I always do my best, sonny boy, thought Gertrude. Don't you worry about that!

"Slang!" she called just before he ducked into his car. "Thanks for being so kind to Lee. You're a gem!"

Slang smiled and gave Gertrude a wave before driving off.

Three things in human life are important. The first is to be kind. The second is to be kind. The third is to be kind.
– Henry James

There is no need for temples; no need for complicated philosophy. Our own brain, our own heart is our temple; the philosophy is kindness.
– Dalai Lama

AND ... CUT TO DOG

Santiago's nose was burning now. Hot, hot, hot, it told her, as she turned onto her own street. Only thing is, that flea was back in her mind again, pestering her with the same old question— "What the heck were you supposed to tell Mom?" And then a clear picture of Lee sprang into her mind, and she could taste his sweet / salty freckles like she'd just licked him a second ago. She came bounding into the yard as Gertrude stood waving goodbye to Slang, and as she galloped toward Gertrude, Santiago remembered exactly what she'd come all this way to tell her. "Woof, woof!" Santiago barked— "Lee loves me again, Mom. He loves me!" Then she went straight to her food bowl, inhaled what was there, and curled up on Lee's bed and went to sleep.

Did you ever stop to think, and forget to start again?
– A. A. Milne

"You can't win 'em all"
– Connie Mack

CUT

WIDE SHOT OF DARKENING FIELD
CATCH LEE'S PROFILE AGAINST RISING MOON

The mind plays tricks on you. You play tricks back!
It's like you're unraveling a big cable knit sweater
that someone keeps knitting and knitting and knitting
and knitting and knitting and knitting …
– Pee Wee Herman

For a while, the panic and danger of the crisis had knocked everything else out of Lee's head. But now, after hours of sitting, and aching, and feeling hopeless, his mind was ready to sock it to him again. Suddenly he was hyper aware of creepy sounds in the long grass—what kind of critters made their homes here, anyway? No doubt, ones with sharp little rodent teeth. Lee shivered. "Get it together, guy," he whispered.

Soon the dark, gloomy feelings of the last couple of weeks started settling around him like a damp, gray army blanket. The sun was starting to set. The mosquitoes were coming out. And as much as he loved Santiago, he didn't really know if she was up to the task. One thing for sure: He didn't feel like listening to Rhonda's voice anymore—and he sure as *heck* didn't have the heart to tell her the rest of the *Old Man* story. I wish Santiago would get here, thought Lee, but what good does wishing ever do? Aaah, what the heck—Lee looked star-ward and whispered a string of words he felt way too old to be reciting: "Star light, star bright ... yadda, yadda ... I wish I may, I wish I might ..."

Rhonda's voice rudely broke his train of wishing.

"As long as there's light at the top of this well," she called, "I'll be okay,"—the rest she barked like a threat—"but if I'm still down here when it gets dark, I'll scream bloody murder, Lee, I really will." In a more trembly voice, she added: "I couldn't take it, Daddy. I just know it!"

"You won't have to," said Lee. "Santiago's got what it takes. She'll be on her way back right now. I can nearly smell her bad breath." He wished he could believe what he was saying. He wished, he wished, he wi—Crud al*mighty*, suddenly an earsplitting scream made him *wish* he'd been wearing earplugs.

"Aaaaaaaaaahh!!Lee!!Yousaidthereweren'tany*spiders*down here!! You promised!! Get off! EEEEEEEUUUUUUWWWWWW!! Get off me!! Ouch, my leg!!"

Lee nearly dropped the bucket. "Calm *down*, Rhonda. You just about gave me a friggin' *heart* attack!"

"You told me they couldn't *breathe* down here. You said there wouldn't be a single one of the ugly, hairy, disgusting, *creepy*, disgusting, *creepy*, scum-sucking, slime-bucket little monsters down here. You lied! You're a big fat liar!" And then she really started to cry—blubber-style.

Lee couldn't take it. "It's going to be all right," he lied.

Rhonda blurted words between sobs. "You're going to be able to hang onto that bucket, aren't you, Daddy? You're not going to let it go, *right*? Tell me you're not going to let it come down on me." It was as if the spider had single-handedly (perhaps *eight*-handedly?) pulled the plug on all her fear.

Lee ached to give her some peace of mind. "Rhonda," he said, piling it on thick, "it's all gonna be okay. I promise. You have to believe me." As he said it, a sense of cold panic spread through his veins and arteries, giving him a strong suspicion that throwing up was about to become an involuntary reflex. Lee swallowed hard.

"No one is coming, Lee," sobbed Rhonda. "Face it. Your arms are going to give out sooner or la—"

"Now *stop* it right there, Rhonda! Do you have any idea who's holding *on*to this bucket?!" He asked so forcefully that Rhonda actually asked the stupidest question of her life:

"Who?"

"Lee McGillicuddy, *that's* who—only the most qualified person on the planet—Lee Bounce-A-Basketball-For-Twelve-Straight-Hours McGillicuddy—Mr. Patience himself." He looked up into the sky. "Ever heard of a guy named Perseus, Ron?"

"No."

Lee counted to ten.

"So, who *is* he?" she called with disgust.

"Beats me," said Lee, "but he said a cool thing: 'He conquers who endures.' Well, I've got endurance comin' out of my butt, Rhonda. I'm more stubborn than the Old Man, for crying out loud. Heck, I might as well *be* the Old Man."

That little performance for Rhonda seemed to suck more energy from Lee than all the bucket-holding in the world. *Crap*, I'm tired. *Soooo* tired. Lee winced from the searing pain of the fishing line cutting trenches into the palms of his hands. *Fish*ing line? Oh, God. That's when Lee's brain got just a tad discombobulated …

> *He settled comfortably against the wood and took*
> *his suffering as it came and the fish swam steadily*
> *and the boat moved slowly through the dark water.*
> *"Fish," he said softly aloud, "I'll stay with you*
> *until I am dead."*
>
> – Ernest Hemingway from The Old Man and the Sea

... Lee felt weirdly dizzy—seasick, almost. He looked at the rope in his hands and felt confused. What's at the other end of this thing ... a fifteen hundred pound—*fish*? ... crap, *am* I the Old Man?!!

Lee closed his eyes and listened to the echo of his absurd question—*am* I? Dude, what's happening to you? But the words were enough to make something click inside his brain—like a light bulb going on. Lee opened his eyes and saw, not a fishing line, but an old rope, holding a very heavy bucket. And then he looked at his bleeding hands—hands that might as well have belonged to Señor Santiago, the stubborn old "I'll Die Before I Let Go Of This Doggone Rope" Man of the Sea.

Lee looked up into the stars that had suddenly become his brothers and his sisters (*yes*, Rhonda), and, of all things ... he laughed—a weak but definite laugh that was only a *tiny* bit delirious. "Okay," he called into the sky. "I get it. Sometimes I'm a little slow, but yeah, I *get* it now!"

"Lee! Who are you talking to?!" called Rhonda.

"Just the Great Director in the sky, Ron ... you wouldn't understand."

"Great *what*?! *Ouch*! Lee, don't tell me you're turning nutcase on me. *Please* don't tell me you're losing it, cuz, like ..."

"Don't worry, Ron," interrupted Lee. "I've never felt saner. Listen, what I was telling you before? It's not just a bunch of hooey. It's the truth! You couldn't be in better hands if you *tried*. Don't you see, Ron? Me and the Old Man, we're tight. We're made of the same damn *stuff*!" Lee smirked in the darkness. "Rhonda," he called, "if you and I were actors in a movie right now, this would go down as the corniest thing ever produced, ya figure?"

"*What?* Daddy, I don't know what kind of *melt*down you're having right now, but do you think you could have it some other ti—"

"Oh, *crud*!" shouted Lee "*Angel* wings!"

"*Angel* wings?!" cried Rhonda. "You're seeing *angels* now? Great. How long till the little pink *ele*phants show up?" Rhonda's irritability was expanding like the inflated throat of a nearby bullfrog, tuning its instrument for the long night ahead.

Lee didn't notice. He was too busy thinking about this morning's Angel Wings e-mail: *May you trust that you are exactly where you were meant to be* ... blah, blah, blah.

"Ron, if I tell you something, do you promise you won't think I'm crazy?"

Too late, thought Rhonda.

"You know all those dumb marathon records I've been putting myself through for years? Do you think it's possible they've been preparing me for this day ... like, you know, *training* me for this exact moment?"

"Get a *grip*, Daddy—" said Rhonda, but Lee cut her off.

"No, really, think about it. If anyone can do this, it's *me*. I could sit here holding onto this tonne-weight till next Christmas if I had to, even if my arms *are* like two squirts of Silly-String. I could pull Moby *Dick* across the ocean in a *dinghy* if I had to. I've got what it takes inside, Rhonda. I'm the one *meant* to be here holding on to this here rope."

And that's all it took. One little thought. One thought, the size of a matchstick, enough to re-ignite his pilot light.

Lee looked up into the stars. "Okay, I'm cool with the script," he whispered. "Let's go with it!"

"... Yeah, yeah," mumbled Rhonda inside her echoing well. "You da man. You could bounce a basketball all the way to the North Pole with a team of reindeer tied to your butt if you had a mind to. What*ever*. Just get me the heck out of this spider-infested hellhole."

"What was that?" called Lee.

"I *said*, 'You da man who's meant to get me out of this *well-hole!*'"

Darn right, thought Lee.

Jeez, could it actually be that simple?

When the solution is simple, God is answering.
– Albert Einstein

CHAPTER TWENTY-SIX

9:14 PM

EXTERIOR OF AGNES'S KITCHEN

GET A SHOT OF THE OLD GAL THROUGH HER KITCHEN WINDOW, THEN FADE TO

THE INSIDE ... ROLL 'EM

Agnes fussed around in the kitchen, re-wiping counters she'd already wiped a dozen times in the last hour. She felt like she had a jar sitting inside her stomach, filled with twenty-five angry hornets—all of them bumping against the glass and each other, knocking themselves out, buzzing their frenzied little brains out. Agnes went to the mirror to check her tongue. She knew it would look fine. This was no tummy bug—just a general uneasy feeling, like something was out of order in her universe.

She went and looked out the window for the tenth time that day, even though she had no idea what she was looking for. On the eleventh trip to the window, she saw Gertrude on her way over. Thank heaven. Someone to talk to.

"Hey, Ag," said Gertrude, "I'm on my way to Shop Smart for some groceries. Anything you're needing?"

"No thanks, Gert." Then she changed her mind. "Then again," she said, "maybe you could pick me up some ginger root. It's good for settling the stomach."

"Tummy troubles?"

"Yes. No. I mean, I don't know. Just nerves, I guess. Would you come in for some tea, Gertrude?"

"Thanks, but no. I want to be back before it gets too dark to do some weeding. I asked Lee to get at those dang dandelions this morning, but I might as well have been whistling into the wind. Guess that's why he vamoosed so fast this morning ... and didn't come home for supper, come to think of it."

Agnes stood on the front steps, watching Gertrude stride down the walk. Suddenly Agnes's mouth blew open. "Gert!"

Gertrude turned around. "What is it, Ag?"

"I'm not ... sure ... I ..." Agnes didn't finish her sentence. Just then, Slang's car pulled up again. He got out and walked up to the two women. "Hey, I was just wondering, was that Lee's dog I saw when I was leaving? 'Cause, like, it occurred to me that wherever Santiago is, Lee's usually not far behind, and I'd like to catch him if ..." Another sentence unfinished.

Gertrude put a firm hand on Slang's arm. "Sorry to interrupt, hon, but I need to go check on something." He and Agnes watched as Gertrude hurried back to her house and came out a second later looking paler than usual.

"Strange," she said. "Santiago's leash is gone. That means Lee has it with him. In which case, why is Santiago here without ..." Another sentence unfinished. They were interrupted by a loud bark coming from the open window of Gertrude's screen door. Santiago had just woken from a bad dream, leaving her with a strange feeling like she'd done something very wrong. She wanted the security of her rhubarb leaves.

FADE TO LEE

Fall seven times, stand up eight.
– Japanese Proverb

And the itsy bitsy spider walked up the spout again.
– Unknown

Up, up and away!
– Superman

Lee's spirits had been down for long enough. *Too* long. Time to get up. He almost felt he could literally *stand* up now and pull the bucket out of the well—with one *hand*, yet. And that's exactly what he did. (Or tried to do.) Of course, the weight of the bucket told him pretty quick that he would do *no such thing*.

In struggling to stand, Lee managed only to shift some more mortar, sending it chinking down on Rhonda.

"*Hey!* What's going on up there, ya big *id*iot?!"

"Sorry 'bout that," called Lee. "Thought I was Superman for a second there."

Lee didn't care if Rhonda was crabby as a hungry dung beetle without a cow paddy in sight. He felt he could put up with even that now.

"Ron? You're not going to sleep, are you?'

"I'm so tired, Daddy."

"No, you're not, Ron. You can't go to sleep now."

"Says who?"

"Says me. I haven't told you the end of the story yet."

Strength does not come from physical capacity.
It comes from an indomitable will.
– Mahatma Gandhi

CHAPTER TWENTY-SEVEN

CUT

NEXT UP, A MONTAGE OF SHORT SCENES BACK TO BACK

START WITH EXTERIOR SHOT OF COP CAR

ZOOM IN ON THE MESS OF BUGS SQUISHED INTO THE FRONT GRILL. ROLL FILM!

Charlotte Bailey sat in the back seat of the cop car, scowling her gorgeous little face off. She had her arms crossed rigidly over her chest (*at least he didn't slap the handcuffs on me*), and looked out the window to avoid the eyes of the cop looking back at her in the driver's mirror.

"Taking me straight to jail?" she snarled.

The policeman just gave his head a shake and sighed. Charlotte rolled her eyeballs until they nearly disappeared, and chewed on her fingernails as she glared out the window. The cop finally spoke up.

"I'm sorry. I really am," he said, "but no daughter of mine is going to hang out on the streets at this time of night. Your mother and I have told you over and over that we expect you home before dark."

"'Hanging out on the streets,'" sneered Charlotte. "You'd think I was a gang member or something. I was just walking around with a few of my friends." She spat a moon-shaped fingernail at the back of the seat in front of her. "Aren't you always telling me to 'get some exercise'?"

"Charlotte," sighed Mr. Bailey, "you're trying my patience."

"How do you think I feel, being dragged off by the cops in front of all my friends?"

"I'm not 'the cops,' Charl," said Mr. Bailey, "I'm your father, and ..."

Charlotte mumbled under her breath. "It's just so embarrassing having a cop for a dad." She looked out the window. "And it isn't even *dark* out!"

Mr. Bailey would have disagreed with that. He clicked on the headlights and looked past the tracks at the darkening fields bordering Wilkes Avenue. He imagined the clouds of mosquitoes swarming in the open grass at this time of night and rolled up the car window. A surprisingly chilly evening for July, he thought. Mr. Bailey looked in the mirror at his daughter. "You didn't bring a cardigan with you?"

"*Cardigan!*" choked Charlotte. "Dad, how *old* are you? Haven't you ever heard of the word *hoodie*?"

"And I suppose you're too cool to wear a swe ..." Mr. Bailey stopped talking and squinted at the road ahead. "*Hel*lo," he said, slowing down, "what have we here?"

"Dad, you're not even on duty!"

Mr. Bailey slowed to a stop. He got out of the car, and instantly started slapping himself silly. Charlotte stayed put, watching her father do the mosquito dance with some satisfaction. Mr. Bailey looked across the empty fields and back at the bikes. "Must be stolen," he said to Charlotte's closed window. He exaggerated the words so she could read his lips. *"I'll just put them in the car and make a report tomorrow."* Charlotte looked away. Her father opened the door a crack. "You'll have to get in the front with your old fuddy-duddy dad, I'm afraid."

Ugh, Charlotte hated it when he said lame things like that. She got out of the car, threw herself in the front seat, and slammed the door shut. Then she went to work killing the twenty thousand or so mosquitoes she'd let in. Mr. Bailey loaded one bike in the trunk, the other in the back seat, and got back in the car, scratching his arms and neck until he left marks. "Lord!" he said. "Those devils could eat a man alive!"

As they drove off, Charlotte turned on the radio to a station that was sure to annoy her dad. She gave a disgusted look at the bike in the back seat, then did a double-take. "Hey."

"What?"

"That ribbon!" Charlotte was hanging over the back seat now, inspecting something tied to the handlebar of the bike. "It's mine!" she said.

Mr. Bailey looked over his shoulder. "A purple ribbon? It could be anyone's."

Charlotte untied the ribbon and sat back down in her seat. "These beads are the ones I sewed on the ends with my own hands, Dad. I oughta know."

"Well?" said her father. "Do you recognize the bike?"

Charlotte shook her head. "Wait a minute," she said, taking another look. "It might be Einstein's."

"That some kind of joke?" asked her father.

"Einstein," repeated Charlotte. "A.k.a., Lee McGillicuddy." She looked out the back window. "That's weird," she said. She watched the telephone poles fly by, one by one, until they each became tiny specks in the night.

TO LEE

KEEP THE SHOTS TIGHT. ROLL!

Dear Lord, be good to me ...
The sea is so wide and my boat is so small.
– Irish Fisherman's Prayer

Lee thought of the Old Man and wondered if mosquitoes existed in Cuba. Lee didn't even have the satisfaction of whacking the bloodthirsty little suckers as they attacked in swarms. He was sure the hateful, stinging bites and burning itchiness pulsating in every part of his body would send him mental. Still, he thought, you could be attacked by worse things than mosquitoes. Try sharks, for example.

"So, Ron," he called, "the Old Man ended up harpooning the fish when it finally came to the surface to jump."

"Killed it dead?" she asked.

"Yeah. And, of course, it was so huge, he couldn't pull it into the boat. He lashed it to the side of the boat with his rope, and he started his long journey home."

"Please tell me he got there," said Rhonda. Lee could hear her teeth chattering. It was starting to get cold.

"Yeah, he got home all right, Ron, but not in the way he'd wanted."

"What happened?" asked Rhonda.

"Sharks," said Lee. "They could smell the fish's blood in the water."

Lee was shivering now, as well.

CUT TO LEE'S HOUSE

LET'S CATCH THIS SHOT BEFORE THE SUN SETS

ROLL!

The way to get started is to quit talking and begin doing.
– Walt Disney

Agnes, Gertrude, and Slang stood in the middle of the sidewalk, looking at one another. Then they all started talking at once:

"Do you think there could be anything wron—"

"What do you suppose we should—"

"When was the last time anyone heard from—"

"I *knew* there was something wron—"

Slang put his hand in the air to stop the jumble of words. "I'm going looking for him."

"I'll come with you," said Gertrude. "Just hang on." She ran to her front door, let Santiago out, and led her to the car. "Lord knows where we'll find him," said Gertrude, stuffing herself and Santiago into the car. "We'll try the park first."

Agnes wrapped her cardigan close and hugged herself. She called to Gertrude. "I'll go inside and wait," she said. "There should be someone here when he gets home."

To keep herself busy, Agnes went about making six loaves of banana bread. She looked at the small jade Buddha on her kitchen windowsill as she mashed the bananas in a large bowl. "He'll be back soon," she whispered to her fat-bellied friend. "He will."

AND ... BACK TO LEE

What you've got here is a perfect eating machine.
It's a miracle of evolution. It does nothing but swim,
eat, and make little sharks.
– From the movie Jaws

"So the sharks came in droves and started taking bites the size of Mr. Woodtick's butt out of the old man's fish."

"That is pretty friggin' big," mumbled Rhonda. "And the poor old guy just had to sit there and watch?"

"Are you kidding?" said Lee. "He clubbed those bloodthirsty thieves with everything he had. He fought so hard, he nearly ended up killing him*self* in the process. But the sharks outnumbered him and, in the end, the Old Man sailed home with nothing more than a huge skeleton lashed to his boat, instead of a beautiful great fish."

Rhonda was silent for a second. "Why are you telling me this, Daddy? Why are you telling me such a sad story?"

"That's just it, Ron. Sure, it was a sad thing that happened to the old man, but here's the bright part: He went home and fell asleep on his newspaper-covered bedsprings, and then the next morning he ... well, he got up. He got *up*, Ron, like he did every day. He rose up out of his bed, all achy and sore, and guess what he did?"

"Do I want to know?" asked Rhonda.

"Yeah, you want to know, Ron," said Lee, and he shifted the rope to a new part of his raw shoulder and began to tell her.

The great majority of men are bundles of beginnings.
– Ralph Waldo Emerson

When the world says, "Give up," Hope whispers,
"Try it one more time."
– Author Unknown

CUT!

DARKNESS QUICKLY DESCENDING

ZOOM IN ON BAILEY

Mr. Bailey parked the police vehicle at the station for the night and unloaded the bikes. Then he and the still-peeved Charlotte got into his van and headed home. Mr. Bailey turned to the country radio station and sang along with gusto …

"… But don't tell my heart / My achy breaky heart / I just don't think it'd understand / And if you tell my heart / My achy breaky …"

Normally this would have been enough to make Charlotte jump

out of the moving vehicle and take her chances, but tonight she was preoccupied.

"Wonder what kind of icing your mom's gonna make for the cake she promised," said Mr. Bailey. Charlotte didn't answer. "I'm awful partial to good old-fashioned butter icing, but you know your mother—she does like to change things up every now 'n' then." He looked over at his silent daughter.

Charlotte's mind was far from frosting. She looked dreamily at the purple ribbon in her hand and found herself thinking about none other than Einstein McGillicuddy.

Mr. Bailey smiled. "A penny for your thoughts?" he said. Charlotte blushed, turned her face to the side window, and looked out into the starry night ... *Star light, star bright, first star I see tonight, I wish I may, I wish I might ...*

CUT

AND OVER TO AGNES

Operator ... Give me the number for 911 ...
– Homer Simpson

I've said it before, and I'll say it again ... aye carumba!
– Bart Simpson

Agnes just about jumped out of her wrinkly skin when the phone rang, sending mashed bananas flying across the kitchen. She lunged for the telephone. "Lee?"

"Just me, Ag," said Gertrude. "He's still not home, eh?"

"No," said Agnes. "I was hoping you'd say he was with *you*. Oh *dear*."

"Now calm down, Agnes," said Gertrude. "There's no reason to panic. You know as well as I do that he's likely off setting some fool record somewhere and lost track of time. Wouldn't be the first time. Now, do me a favor, Ag, and go over to my house and do your waiting there. I want someone around in case he phones. Oh, and Ag? Grab a pencil and take down Slang's cell number."

Agnes scribbled down the number and forgot to say goodbye before hanging up. She threw on her cardigan and hustled over to Gertrude's house in the dark. She found the key in its usual hiding place under an old cowboy boot with flowers growing out the top. She had a heck of a time keeping her hand steady as she tried to get the key in the lock. She didn't even notice the mosquitoes feasting on her bare ankles.

When she was finally inside, Agnes didn't like the empty feel of Gertrude's house. The heavy, in-your-face silence made her uneasy. When the phone suddenly knifed the air with its unexpected ring, Agnes just about knocked her head on the ceiling. With a hand over her beating heart, she picked up the telephone. "Yes?!!" she screeched.

"Mrs. Gertrude McGillicuddy? This is Police Constable Charlie Bailey speaking." Agnes's knees gave way and she sank onto the couch. "Yeah, I picked up a couple of abandoned bikes on Wilkes Avenue this evening, and I have reason to believe that one of them may be your son's. Has his bike been stolen recently?"

"Jesus, Mary, and Joseph!" shrieked Agnes into the police constable's ear and promptly hung up on him. She reached into her pocket for Slang's cell number, grabbed for the phone, and just as she touched it, it began to ring. "Mary, and all the angels in heaven!!" Again, she clutched her heart as she spoke into the receiver. "Lee?! Is that you, Sonny?"

"Gertrude?" came a voice at the other end.

"No, it's Agnes, and I have to hang up now, so ..."

"Agnes," said Mr. Ronaldson, "it's Reg, from across the street. I was just wondering if either you or Gert have seen Rhonda around lately. She's been gone all day and she missed her music lesson which is very unusual for—"

"Reginald," cut in Agnes, "you'd best get over here right now." Slam.

Agnes flubbed the phone number twice before finally getting through to Slang's cell. Gertrude answered.

"Gert," said Agnes with a shaky voice, "Lee's bike ... the police found it abandoned on Wilkes Avenue ... and Rhonda is missing, too ... Gertrude, I'm worried ..." She heard Gertrude telling Slang to put his foot on the gas and get them over to Wilkes Avenue. This time it was Gertrude's turn to hang up without saying goodbye.

"Gertrude!" shouted Agnes into the receiver. "I want to come with you!" The only answer was a dismal dial tone.

CUT

PAN THE DARKENING FIELD AND ZOOM IN
ON THE ROPE BURNS ON LEE'S SHOULDER

"The old man slept hard," said Lee, "and then he got up out of bed, Ron, and what does the old guy do?"

"Skip the guessing games, Lee."

"He started making plans for the next day's fishing, *that's* what he did," said Lee. "He didn't stay down, Ron. He got back up."

"Was he nuts?"

"No, he was a hero." Lee looked up at the stars and the moon. "Don't you see, Ron? He took all his crappy disappointment and pain and recycled it."

"Into what?"

"Into *fuel* ... to keep on ... well, you know ..."—Lee was about to use the word "loving," but remembered who he was talking to—"to keep on *living*. To keep his flame burning."

Rhonda was silent for a time. "I can see the moon, Lee," she said finally. "Where's Santiago?"

Lee didn't answer. He was looking at the moon as well, thinking of … gorgeous Charlotte Bailey, of all people. It had suddenly slipped into his mind that he'd give his right arm to one day sit beneath this very same moon with her and talk about the books they'd read.

Fat chance. He had a strong suspicion he'd be forced to keep both his arms. Sigh.

Love is a smoke made with the fume of sighs.
– William Shakespeare

Nothing takes the taste out of peanut butter
quite like unrequited love.
– Charlie Brown

CUT!

LONG SHOT OF SLANG'S VEHICLE KICKING UP DUST ON THE DIRT ROAD

ZOOM IN ON PASSENGER SIDE AND SECURE A GOOD SHOT OF DOG'S CLAWS

SCRATCHING DAYLIGHTS OUT OF WINDOW

ROLL!

When Slang turned onto Wilkes Avenue, Santiago, who'd been whimpering in the back seat, sat up and started yelping. Her nose was telling her something. It was *hot*. And getting hotter every second. She was getting closer and closer … to what? And then it all came flooding back: Lee, his sweet and salty freckles, Rhonda's voice down a deep hole, the baseball cap, *bring Mom back, bring Mom back*.

Santiago leapt to the front seat, onto Gertrude's lap, and started barking out the window.

"What is it, girl?" said Gertrude.

Santiago's nose continued to get hotter until she felt like she might explode if she didn't get out of the car *right now. Right this very minute!* She started pawing wildly at the window and barking in Gertrude's face.

"Stop the car, Slang," said Gertrude. "Santiago's trying to tell us something."

CUT TO INTERIOR OF BAILEY HOME

The only real valuable thing is intuition.
– *Albert Einstein*

"Charlotte, honey," said Mr. Bailey, "it's pitch black out, and swarming with monster mosquitoes. What good could it possibly do to go out there now?"

"It's just that it doesn't make any sense," said Charlotte. "Lee's bike is too crappy for anyone to bother stealing."

"And you think he's in some kind of trouble?"

"I don't know. It's just a *feeling*," said Charlotte. "I just think we should take a look around, is all."

Mr. Bailey put down his untouched slice of chocolate cake with vanilla butter icing, sighed, and looked at Mrs. Bailey. His wife shrugged. "Might be best to listen to Charlotte's intuition, love," she said. "It won't take long to have a look around. Bring your high-powered flashlight along."

Mr. Bailey could never refuse Mrs. Bailey anything, especially when she called him "love." He and Charlotte covered themselves in long sleeves and bug spray and went back out into the night. The crunching of gravel under rubber as Mr. Bailey backed out of the driveway momentarily drowned out the sound of frogs singing in the ditches. As the rumble of the car faded into the distance, hundreds of slick green bodies again filled the darkness with frog-song.

COMING UP ON A SERIES OF SHORT SNIPPETS

LET'S KEEP THE CAMERA WORK TIGHT AND THE PACE QUICK

WE'LL TAKE FIVE TO REAPPLY BUG SPRAY AND THEN WE'RE ROLLIN'!

Success seems to be largely a matter of hanging on
after others have let go.
– William Feather

Lee let out an involuntary groan. Mosquitoes had bitten both his eyelids, and they were itchy and swollen. The urge to free up his hands and scratch the living daylights out of every part of his body was almost too much to bear.

"What's the matter?" asked Rhonda, sounding frightened. "Are you okay?"

"I'm fine," said Lee. But he was far from fine. The cramps in his hands had gone past pain to a numb dullness he didn't trust. If he couldn't feel his hands, how would he know if he was still hanging on tight enough?

"Are you sure?" said Rhonda. "Are you sure you're okay?"

"Relax, Ron. We haven't been here for even close to twelve hours yet. I've broken harder and longer records than this." Lee squeezed his eyes shut and tried with all his might to hold back another groan of pain.

If you wanna catch a big fish, son, you need desire
and stubborn determination by the truckload.
– Frankindad McGillicuddy

CUT!

Santiago exploded out of the car when Gertrude opened the door and shot off into the blackness like a hound after a rabbit. "Hold on, girl!" said Gertrude, nearly tripping over the shin-high wire fence in the dark. "Wait for us!"

CUT!

"I think this is about where we found the bikes," said Charlotte, peering into the glow cast by the headlights.

"Oh, it's '*we*' now, is it?" said Mr. Bailey, smiling to himself in the dark. "An hour ago, I was the worst old fuddy-duddy in the world for insisting on stopping."

"Dad," moaned Charlotte, "do you think you could stop using that word? *Hey* … there's a car parked up there. And look! There's people running!"

Mr. Bailey stopped smiling and assumed his serious "Police Constable" face.

"I think you should stay in the car, honey," he said to Charlotte, as he jerked the car to a stop.

CUT!

Lee knew he was starting to get delirious now. He imagined he heard the bark of a dog. A dog that sounded just like Santiago. "Get a hold of yourself, Lee," he whispered into the night. "This is no time for your imagination to make a fool out of you."

CUT!

Agnes poked the back of the cab driver's neck and told him for the tenth time to put his foot on the gas. "This is an *emergency*, young man. Don't you understand?!" she shrieked.

Mr. Ronaldson tried to calm her. "Agnes, he's going as fast as he—" But he let out an "Ouch!" instead of finishing. Agnes had her fingernails digging into his wrist. Reginald Ronaldson was almost glad his wife was away on business—if he'd been sandwiched between both women, he'd have *two* lacerated wrists by now.

"Look up ahead," shouted Agnes, digging her nails in deeper. "There's a couple of cars parked on the shoulder. And one of them's a cop car! Oh, *Lordy*, my stomach is telling me there's something awfully wrong here."

CUT!

"Lee!" cried Rhonda, "Was that a bark I—"

"No, Ron, it's just—" but the next yelp told him loud and

clear that this was no trick of the imagination.

"Santiago?! Santi?" He couldn't say another word, because the sound of his dog's voice was sending tears down his mosquito-ravaged cheeks.

CUT!

Agnes went flying, "arse over teakettle" (as she liked to say), when she hit the wire fence, but Mr. Ronaldson pulled her up like a yo-yo and they ran like fiends to where a crowd was forming. Agnes saw Gertrude on her knees in the grass, holding a limp rag doll that just happened to be Lee. Slang had hold of God-knows-what on the end of a rope and was using every muscle in his body to pull it up out of what? … an old well, while Constable Bailey punched the numbers 911 into his cell phone. Mr. Ronaldson rushed to Slang's side.

"She's down there," groaned Slang, pulling at the bucket. "There's a girl at the bottom of the well."

Mr. Ronaldson took hold of the rope and started hauling it out like it weighed two pounds. "Ron, girl, you *okay*, honey?" he called. "Are you all *right,* angel?!"

By now, Rhonda was blubbering again and they couldn't understand much of what she said—something about "leg," and "*spider*," and "get me *outa* here!!"

CHAPTER TWENTY-EIGHT

{
We never know how high we are
Till we are called to rise
And then if we are true to plan
Our statures touch the skies
– Emily Dickinson
}

Lee relaxed against the comfort of his mother's strong arms and looked up into the stars. She was saying things to him, asking him questions, but, for the moment, words were nothing compared to the pull of the stars and the moon. His body felt the same way his arms once did after trudging home from the store with the Christmas grocery bags loaded with a twenty-five-pound turkey and two ten-pound bags of potatoes—when he finally put the bags down, his arms felt like they might float right up to the ceiling, regardless of what plans he might have for them. The same sensation filled him now. Lee felt that his body might float all the way to the moon if he let it.

By the time the paramedics arrived, Lee was feeling a little more anchored—back in the real world, where mosquitoes had no intention of letting him forget he had a body.

"Here, let's put this blanket around him," said one of the paramedics to Gertrude. Lee scratched at his swollen eyelids. Ouch. He asked Santiago to lick his face, and her gentle tongue made him remember how he used to believe that Santiago's spit could cure him of anything, if necessary. The paramedic gently pulled Santiago away from Lee's face, gave her a gentle pat on the rump—*"you're a beauty, aren't you?"*—and turned his attentions to Lee. He examined Lee's eyes, checked his pulse, asked him some questions.

"How many fingers do you see? Are you injured anywhere? Have you had any food or water since this morning?" He whistled when he saw Lee's raw hands and shoulder. "Mama Mia. How long have you been sitting there holding that bucket, buddy?"

"Close to twelve hours, I'm guessing," croaked Lee.

"Good Lord, where did you find the strength?"

Lee winced as the paramedic applied ointment to his wounds and insect bites with kind and caring hands. Then the man smiled, tousled Lee's hair, and asked if he felt strong enough to stand up and make it to the ambulance.

"I'm staying right here," said Lee. "I'm not moving an inch till Rhonda's out."

Gertrude and Agnes hovered around him, touching his cheek, his forehead, rubbing his blanket-covered arms to keep him warm, whispering how brave he'd been, how amazing he was. Santiago rested her chin and one paw on Lee's lap, as if to claim ownership. *"This is* my *boy. This is the boy who loves me."*

Slang went missing for a minute or two, but came sprinting back from his car with the team shirt held between his hands like a victory flag. "You're number one, kid," he said, and just about gave Lee the usual punch in the shoulder before remembering it might not be such a good idea.

But then Lee saw an apparition that made him wonder if he was still in la-la-land after all. She appeared out of nowhere. Gorgeous Charlotte Bailey. Yep, I'm hallucinating, for sure, thought Lee, but he didn't mind. Not one little bit. Lee noted that Charlotte looked even *more* gorgeous in his hallucinations. Like an angel. She didn't say a word. She just knelt down beside him, gave him a smile he would never forget, then took his hand and placed something in it. He looked down to find himself holding Charlotte's purple hair ribbon—the one from his bicycle handlebar. "Hey!" he called, but Charlotte was already slipping back into the shadows. Mr. Bailey looked over his shoulder, but Charlotte gave Lee the "quiet" sign with one finger on her lips, and ran off in the direction of the car.

> *Just when I think that I'm alone*
> *It seems there's more of us at home*

There's a multitude of angels,
And they're playing with my heart.
– Annie Lennox

Without love, what are we worth? Eighty-nine cents! Eighty-
nine cents' worth of chemicals, walking around lonely.
– Hawkeye Pierce, M*A*S*H

CHAPTER TWENTY-NINE

Lee guessed that Rhonda was just too tired to be cranky anymore, because she quietly cooperated with the rescue paramedic who first lowered himself into the well (Lee couldn't figure out how a grown man and a girl could fit down a well together in the first place, let alone have enough room to get her rigged up in a harness), and as she was slowly lifted out, even her "ouches" were subdued. Her face looked like a pale, pale moon against the darkness as it rose out of the well, and, for once in her life, she appeared speechless.

Mr. Ronaldson fussed and cooed over her like she was a baby; in fact, that's exactly what he called her every two seconds—"You okay, baby? Everything's going to be all right, sugar baby. Come on, babes, we're just about there." Lee was surprised Rhonda didn't bite her dad's head off for calling her that in public. Instead, she just collapsed into his arms as soon as he was able to cradle her dangling body, harness and all. Lee went over to pat her on the shoulder, and she surprised him again by not only giving him a hug, but hanging on tight an extra second or two before letting go. "Thanks," she whispered. "Ouch. Ow."

Good thing it was dark. "Hey, anytime, Rhonda," said Lee, blushing.

"My name's not ... Ow! *Ouch*!"

CHAPTER THIRTY

EVERYBODY READY?

OKAY, JUST RELAX

SOMEONE GET THE DOG TO STOP LICKING HER BUTT

GOOD. WE'RE LOOKING GOOD ... ROLL TAPE

Lee stood before the lens of the television camera, trying not to grin from ear to ear, but he was having difficulty with the modesty thing. And why not? Wasn't every day he stood in front of a local television camera for an interview. He fidgeted with Santiago's leash as the news reporter spoke into the camera.

"Thirteen-year-old Lee Einstein McGillicuddy, of 933 Dorchester Avenue, received a special medal of honor, presented by Manitoba's Lieutenant Governor at a ceremony held on the legislative grounds this morning. McGillicuddy spent a grueling twelve and a half hours averting certain catastrophe by preventing the fall of a rock-filled bucket, dangling above the body of a young girl trapped in an abandoned well. Eleven-year-old Rhonda Ronaldson had accidentally fallen into the well, sustaining a broken leg and mild concussion.

"Lee," said the journalist, turning to Lee with the mike, "how does it feel to be a hero?"

"Well, I don't know about heroism, Greg," laughed Lee, "but I think I may have broken a world record for sustaining the most mosquito bites per square inch of exposed human flesh. I plan to look into it."

Greg chuckled. "I understand you have a special interest in breaking records," he said. "How do you plan to top this one?"

Lee grinned at Rhonda, who stood beside him, sporting a full leg cast and a couple of crutches. "I'm thinking of bouncing a basketball all the way to the North Pole with a team of reindeer tied to my butt," he said. "And Rhonda here, she's going to be my manager."

Rhonda grabbed the mike from Greg and spoke into the camera. "For the record, my name's not Rhonda, it's *Ron*. And yeah, I'll be selling tickets to the event. Ten bucks, if you're interested."

Greg smiled as he recovered the mike from Rhonda and spoke directly into the camera. "Inspired by this young duo's indomitably bright spirit, this reporter, for one, intends to buy a ticket! This is Greg Stanley for WYG news. And now, over to you, Roger, for a close-up look at the weather."

CUT!

Gertrude and Agnes stood off to the side, beaming, as only two proud mothers can. They watched as Lee joked with the cameraman after the interview and asked if he could hold the camera on his own shoulder, just to see how it felt. He winced as the camera came to rest on his scarred shoulder, but even then it felt good.

"It suits you!" joked the cameraman.

"I'd have to gain a few more pounds to carry around *this* mama," said Lee, handing the heavy camera back.

"How much you weigh, anyway, kid? You're the skinniest beanpole I've ever seen ..."

Gertrude smiled at the two of them chatting and laughing. "Agnes," she whispered, "your suggestion about the two of us giving the kid a gift to let him know we're proud? I've think I've got an idea ..."

CHAPTER THIRTY-ONE

{
**Catch the trade winds in your sails.
Explore. Dream. Discover.**
– Mark Twain
}

Santiago nuzzled her nose beneath the spread out Camcorder instructions that Lee had had his nose buried in for the last hour. Lee smiled, put the instruction booklet down on the back stoop, and gave his dog all the ear-scratching, tummy-rubbing attention she deserved.

"Let's go inside, girl," he said when the breeze began to chill. Santiago's claws scrabbled against the wooden back steps as she scrambled to the door ahead of Lee, imagining the bedtime snack that awaited inside. Lee took one last look into the sky and panned the expanse of twinkling stars, using his fingers as a fake lens for the very last time. "Goodnight, Einstein," he whispered. "Night, Dad."

Goodnight, McGillicuddy!
– Albert

Buona notte, Señor McGillicuddy

– Leonardo da Vinci

Your stature reaches the sky, Lee. Star-kissed dreams, my friend.

– Emily

Night, Kid!

– Groucho

Good night, Master McGillicuddy.

– William Shakespeare

Goodnight, friend.

– Mark Twain

Kalinishta, Lee.

– Plato

Sweetest of Dreams, Lee.

– William Blake

Keep smiling, Lee.

– Charlie Chaplin

Bliss, Lee.

– Buddha

Keep your ears screwed on tight, Lee.

– Vincent

sleep your dreams / dream your sleep.

– e. e. cummings

Jo tau, Mista Ree!

– Confucius

You dared to take the road less traveled. You go, guy!!

– Robert Frost

Hit a homer in your dreams, McGillicuddy!

– Cornelius McGillicuddy

INTERVIEW WITH
COLLEEN SYDOR

It's a pretty obvious question but where did the idea for this intriguing story spring from?

I remember seeing an illustration once of a boy standing on the edge of a barn roof with outstretched arms on which he was wearing a large pair of homemade, rather suspect-looking wings. That picture stayed with me. It spoke of longing and a burning, youthful desire. It spoke about believing and "wanting" to the max. In *The McGillicuddy Book of Personal Records*, Lee knows that his personal records mania is only a stepping stone on the way to "becoming." The fact that he doesn't know exactly what that will be only serves to make him more tenacious and I find this a very positive and endearing character trait.

Lee and Rhonda are different ages and different genders; yet they have a strong, though unstated, friendship. Do you think this kind of relationship occurs a lot between boys and girls of these ages?

I think that in the general mainstream scheme of things, this kind of relationship does not exist in great numbers (probably because of unspoken gender and age related rules and expectations). However, often kids are "thrown together," for example as cousins or family friends or, as in the case of Lee, by proximity. Rhonda lives across the street from him. Since they're both stubborn and independent, they gravitate toward one another and the friendship—albeit outwardly grudging—develops naturally.

Lee is in many ways a lone wolf. He doesn't have a lot of friends his own age, and yet he has a strongly focused life, and doesn't seem lonely. Do you think there are a lot of Lees in this world, who pursue their own interests without appearing to need companionship?

Yes. And I am one of them. That's probably why I'm an author. I'm able to do my work for the most part by myself. It takes a lot of different kinds of people with different needs and inclinations to make the world tick. Sometimes I fall into the trap of feeling a little bad or "unusual" about not needing a large social network. Then I give my head a shake and paint a picture or write a story and know that I'll surface when I'm ready. My friends are patient with me.

Rhonda is a feisty, complicated character. While this is primarily Lee's story, Ron is almost as interesting as he is. What is her place in the story?

Rhonda never started out having a specific agenda or "place" in the story. She simply appeared as I started writing and I couldn't deny her a depth of character. She is secondary, but she came to me alive and breathing and I didn't want to stifle her verve. I really like Rhonda.

In your story, you give the adult characters more than a one-dimensional role in the story. Why did you choose to do that?

Again, I didn't "choose" consciously to bring dimension to the roles of the adults in the book. But I find colorful characters more interesting to read and write about. Also, as I'm writing, I can't help listening to how the characters wish to be presented. Writing has a lot to do with a certain kind of intuitive "listening." I know this sounds a bit goofy but it delights me when I start "hearing" their voices and hence their roles instead of forcing them to life.

What about Santiago's role?

It seemed natural to me that since Santiago is such a big part of Lee's life, he also needed a "voice." I've never owned a dog but I imagine that dogs, cats, any kind of living being that's important to someone else, must have the same tinges of compassion, joy, and empathy that we as humans experience. I know this is a little anthropomorphic, but that's the fun and poetic freedom of being an author. I say what goes—unless my editor suggests I rethink. In this case, I know my editor is a dog lover and perhaps that's what saved Santi's unusual depiction in this book!

One reader of this book compares the story to those written by Mark Twain. Whether that's true or not, both Lee and Rhonda are given the freedom to discover their world so that they can have independent adventures that help to strengthen and enlarge their characters. Do you think we need to give young people more independence so that they can realize their potential?

Absolutely! It seems we often hear the old sentence that begins: "Back when I was a kid …"—words that usually tell stories of kids free to adventure together, not needing or particularly desiring the presence of adults in their neighborhood networks.

Within reason, I think it's healthy for kids to be intensely with other kids to the extent that they forget they have parents and care-givers. Being lost in "play" and discovering independently and unabashedly has to be a good thing, I think.

You've used some of the conventions of film and TV scene-setting as the story develops. Why?

Just as I "hear" what my characters wish to say, I often "see" scenes unfolding like a movie being played just for me. With this book, I completely gave in to the idea of fast-moving movie scenes and I used a director's voice to allow the reader to also "see" the scenes unfolding. Usually a book is written from the point of view of only one character, but this technique allowed me to achieve multiple perspectives and even have some of the various scenes happening simultaneously. The director's voice helped make the transition between perspectives clear and obvious. I also felt that this would appeal to the young readers of today who are used to, and delighted by, fast-paced media of all sorts.

In this story you have been able to skillfully blend the comic and the dramatic. How does that mix reflect your own view of the world?

When I go to a movie, for example, I am particularly drawn to scenes where something intended to be funny makes me feel sad, or something sad can make me laugh. I think this has something to do with willingness (on both the viewer and the character's part) to be vulnerable—to remember that sometimes our underwear is showing and it's okay.

What advice would you give to young writers?

Love lots, fear nadda, and WRITE!!

Colleen Sydor was born and raised in Winnipeg, where she lives with her husband and three children. She brings quick wit and a lively sense of language to her books for young readers. Four of her books have won the McNally Robinson Book For Young People award. Sydor's children have always been grist for her writer's mill. She finds that as they grow in feet and inches, so her stories are lengthening as well. *The McGillicuddy Book of Personal Records* is her second novel for young adults.